FALL:

Lucifer Morning Star

The Fallen Chronicles: Book One

D.S. Hay

CLARA LOUISE HAY
RETURNING THE FAVOR

D.S. Hay

ACKNOWLEDGMENTS

With humble acknowledgement to the works of Gaiman, Brust, Martin, Tolkien, Ripley, Clancy, Ellis, Barker, Moore, Davidson, and Schroeder.

ALPHA

I have no doubt the earth has never known thunder like this. I shudder as it echoes through my body and mind, hammering out a permanent memory, like repeated blows on a blacksmith's anvil.

God save us

And although this tale deals with beings of a higher nature, we may see that— ~~these beings were the templates for humans and *may* find within them the origin of our essence.~~

~~Our humanity.~~

We are not like them, O Lord

~~I've learned that we are closer to God than we believe,~~ ~~and~~ to shun

1

this story as fantastical or whimsy is a dangerous choice; one that may, ~~in time, darken the mirror of that most overlooked and precious of commodities.~~

destroy before Creation

The *neshama.*

Our souls.

turned

As the thunder fades, and the stench of decaying flesh and rotting wood mixes, one thing seems clear. ~~We do have a choice. Even those branded unredeemable now realize that salvation may end with a Supreme Being, but must begin within ourselves.~~

The End is now.

For he is dead...

Have You truly forsaken us?

If, in fact, a morning star can rise to the heavens...

I pray the Lord my soul to take before now

--Margaret McCreedy
Eden, somewhere west of
Lake Turkana

2

ONE: *A VISITOR*

THE STRANGER appeared one afternoon, on the eve of the Ritual of Flight. Duma, having a mischievous (and what some would whisper lazy) streak, had decided not to join his brothers in the weekly outing. Instead, he chose to walk, his wings folded tightly against his back like a bird's wings in winter. He trod upon a dirt path over a few hills down to the Southern Slope of Heaven. The Field of Gold rippled gently like an amber sheet in the breeze, and the Presence was quite warm upon his face. He liked it here; it always seemed more peaceful than anywhere else. Duma preferred to work alone, but his assignments in the Silver City often required the cooperation of several of his brothers. Generally, he got along with most whether they be of the Sarim or Cherubim.

But he never passed up an opportunity to sneak away, which he often did. And although he would lightly be punished, he would gladly make up for his "indiscretions" with extra chores. Duma's temperament was unpredictable and his brothers did not complain when he missed the Flight. In fact, some were quite glad he did not join in the Ritual. Most of them could recall a certain time or two when Duma flew too close or plucked from them a feather here and there and then laughed at them.

But Duma cared for none of their whisperings. It paled in comparison to what he'd been called six thousand years ago. Most of the angels had forgotten or acted as though it had never happened.

Ridiculous. ⟶

Four centuries ago a younger naive angel named Cassiel had called him a rebel, and Duma, in a frenzied attack gouged out Cassiel's left eye but broke one of his own wings in the melee.

It was a painful memory. Made more so perhaps by the fact that only one of his brothers, the archangel Ramiel, stepped forward to protest Duma's punishment on the rack. But soon after the Sopheriel twins, along with the Irin and Qaddism who constitute the supreme judgment council or *beth din,* saw fit to amend the Law of Heaven, citing that the rack was no longer appropriate punishment for one of the Host. A historic decision, but one that did nothing for

Duma and the faint circle of scars on his feet, ankles and wing blades.

But all that matters not, he tried to convince himself. The wing had healed with time, though it was now not quite as strong as it had once been. Instead, he discovered his love for simply walking, and for being alone.

Duma crested the hill and veered off onto a narrow path into the Field of Gold. The path was no wider than was absolutely necessary, and Duma was always careful to either tuck his wings in extremely tight or to raise them like two great sails above the tops of the thin amber stalks.

He walked several hundred yards to his favorite spot. It was a clearing in the field worn by the diameter of his wings, roughly twenty feet across. He stooped to one knee and touched the dirt. It was cool and slightly yielding to his touch. Perfect with the warmth of the Presence. He flapped his wings thrice, and the resulting wind eased the wheat at the edge of the circle outward, giving a wider view of sky as he lay on his back. Soon his brothers would take flight in the bright sky, like bats spilling into the dusk. Duma closed his eyes and waited for the beating of his brothers' wings.

∞

He awoke to a great whooshing sound. The sky was clear, the light had shifted. Had he slept through the Flight? He did not think so. He rubbed the sleep from his eyes and sat up.

Again there was a great whoosh.

Duma felt a small buzzing at the base of his neck. His wing throbbed where it had set badly. His head swam for a moment.

He raised his head above the level of the wheat. Something caught his eye. A figure on the road. His dirt road. Similar wings. At first he could not see the face, but the movements were lithe and graceful. And not recognizable. The stranger lifted his arms and wings, moving through a short series of motions. He held his face up to the light as Duma had done so only hours before. And then Duma saw...

The buzz traveled down his spine, and when it hit his feet, he tore off through the Field of Gold stooped over, trampling stalks and crushing the chaff under his feet. The stalks whipped and flayed his arms, his face and wings. The panic was uncontrollable. When he broke free of the clearing onto another dirt path he took flight, the old wound forgotten. Ligaments strained and creaked, and an airborne Duma raced back towards the Silver City.

The rhythm of flight came back to him easily, as did the pain. He chanced a look over his shoulder, but could see nothing. His smooth skin began to crawl.

He's behind me, he's right behind me.

Duma flew faster, pushing himself. At the edge of the Silver City his adrenaline wore off. Fatigue and cramps turned muscles into balls of steel. He crash-glided to the paved street a mile away from the First Grand Spire (whose entrance was forbidden to Duma). His muscles were so fatigued that he could not completely fold his wings; they bounced and scraped the pavement as he willed his legs to worker faster. He stumbled at the top of the First Grand Spire's stairs and lost his balance, smashing his mouth and bloodying it. He stumbled to his feet and heaved through the two great double doors.

"Ramiel, RAMIEL, *RAMIEL!*"

Immediately, two angels swooped down upon him and easily wrestled him to the ground.

Duma spit blood, a scarlet thread between his lip and the granite floor. "Ramiel!"

The archangel Uriel looked down at Duma and nudged his ribs with a sandaled foot. "You are forbidden to enter the Spire, Little Rebel, and Ramiel is not here to defend you."

"*RAMIEL!*" Duma's voice echoed throughout the spire.

Several angels stopped their tasks and turned to the disturbance.

"*HeishereheishereIsawhim.*"

"Saw whom, Duma?"

7

"He's come home. The Prince has come home."

Uriel bent down and caught Duma's gaze at eye level. Touched Duma's lip with a slim finger. The bleeding stopped. "What Prince is this?"

"The First of the Fallen."

TWO: *THE WRITER*

ANOTHER STREAK. In the split second it took Margaret McCreedy to look up, it was gone.

Third tonight.

She turned back to her pad and pen, the end of which was indented with numerous bite marks. She leaned forward over her wooden desk and shut the window. The air had grown chilly, and the bugs were starting to annoy her, but she loved the faint symphony of crickets and the accompanying odd sounds from the woods outside her cabin. An earth-toned palate threatened to shake loose from the trees near the porch, and she looked forward to having to break out the rake. It gave her an excuse to get away from her pads and pens and out of the house.

On her desk sat an old Royal typewriter she'd had

since college— which was a considerable time ago, but it had served her well, and she in turn had remained faithful to it. But it seemed this week the typewriter preferred silence. As the week before and the week before that.

She turned her attention to a framed black and white photo now yellowed with age. It was a young man in his late teens in dress blues. The picture was supposed to be serious, but she could see the smile barely being constrained behind his sharp eyes. The lettering below read: PVT. HAROLD C. MCCREEDY, USMC.

The phone rang, a harsh analog bell. She turned down her hearing aid and picked up on the second ring. "Nobody I know would be calling this late."

Laughter from the other side. "Maggie, darling, I knew you would be up churning out the most delicious glitzy trash."

"I can't get a goddamn thing done you keep calling me."

Her hands ached from the phone already so she popped a few painkillers and washed them down with a finger of Glenfiddich.

"Look, darling. I know you relish the invasion and I would join you up there in the woods, but I have this thing about bugs, and well the publisher called me. At home. Wanted to know how the new Sapphire was coming. Is she or is she not going to marry Lord Sterling?"

Maggie looked to the spot on her desk, which faithfully over the years had supported a thick pile of yellow legal notepads. Tonight there were two.

"Great, it's going great."

"How's your arthritis? Do I need to hire you another assistant?"

"Should be finished in two weeks."

"Well is she, or is she not? I hope—"

Maggie clicked the receiver home and unplugged it. "Yeah, so do I."

She leaned back in her chair and pulled a cigar out of the top drawer, nipped the end with a pair of scissors. She chewed on one end, thoughtfully. The new Sapphire book was done, the ten notepads stacked haphazardly by the couch, where they'd sat for a few weeks. But Maggie was hoping to finish another book.

A better one.

Sapphire, the professional damsel in distress, was what they call in the publishing business a midlist book. Which meant she had over the course of fifteen years gained about 90,000 readers. A respectable number; it allowed her the luxury of a small ranch in Wisconsin and a continuous supply of Cubans.

She coughed harshly and chided herself for leaving the window open so long with the chill. She hawked a load of the brown stuff into a handkerchief and tossed it into the trashcan.

She loved Sapphire, and Sapphire had been good to her. What started out as a bet with a friend ended up a sold book, and then another and then another and another. But Sapphire was growing old, as was she. She had discussed this with a fellow writer in Maine after reading a book of his about a romance writer in a similar situation. His advice, given half-jokingly, was "kill the whore."

The wind blew a leaf against the window, scratching it like a whispered conversation.

Her publishers hoped that the next book was going to be her breakout book, a book that would jump her sales into the 200,000 range. She really didn't care for all the marketing and number crunching that went into the books. She used to make so much fun of her girlfriends' books that on a dare she actually read one, eschewing Monday Night Football with her husband. The following night she sat down at her old typewriter and copied one word for word. This allowed her to get the feel, pacing and length of the story. Then she opted to switch the plot around in so much as those plots can be switched and added a little sparkle and color to the characters. The next thing she knew she had a three book deal, and Sapphire became a real friend.

She almost didn't sign, but with her friends encouraging her she put her signature on the dotted line and found she rather enjoyed writing, although she felt a little bit of guilt each time she cashed a check. But as Harold was fond of pointing out, it was a feeling she quickly got over.

But she was stuck now. Writer's block, some called it. When this demon would rise she would normally call one of her friends and listen to outlandish situations and ideas that they were more than willing to suggest, hoping to make it to the Special Thanks page. When that didn't work, she pictured her readers in her head.

She would imagine them all sitting in a high school gym and think to herself, they all read my book, this number of people scattered over the USA and overseas. And they want to hear a story. So just sit down and tell them one. And then the next Sapphire book would come.

Usually.

The new one by the couch contained Sapphire's answer to Lord Sterling's proposal. It would surprise the readers— if it got past her editor.

The door blew open with a bang, and Maggie jumped, almost falling out of her chair. She went to the door, pulling her flannel shirt closer and poked her head outside and looked around. The ring of light from the porch light extended only a few yards past the flowerbed. She saw nothing and closed the door, double checking that she had locked it.

More leaves swirled outside her window.

Sapphire, she thought. A million words about you, and I haven't said anything important.

And fall is coming.

THREE: *REACQUAINTANCE*

THE FIRST GRAND SPIRE was constructed so as to make the most use of natural light from an intricate array of windows and skylights. During this time of the day the light fell in shafts spotlighting the floor, but leaving no small amount of the spire's hall in darkness. Dust particles floated like tiny snowflakes ignoring the laws of gravity.

Prince Lucifer Morning Star stepped forward into the Hall. Whereas most angels had a fleshier softness to their bodies, Lucifer's was trim and compact, muscles defined sharply like an athlete's. He stood taller than most angels, and projected an arrogant, yet charismatic air. Would you expect any less from such a creature? He stood within inches of the kneeling Duma. The moment Lucifer's foot touched the darkness, it scattered and the Grand Hall was lit from within.

Now all the angels stopped their tasks. Some landed awkwardly on the floor itself, shielding their eyes with raised arms; others perched on ledges and forced themselves into alcoves, hoping for the cover of darkness but finding none. The air grew still as the last echoes of ruffled feathers and hurried conversations dissipated.

Another angel appeared at the bottom of an elaborate spiral staircase that disappeared far above. He was taller than all the others. As he walked with steady, almost hurried steps, the air seemed to part several feet ahead of him.

"Good afternoon, Mika'il."

"Light Giver," Michael said. "You are late for the Ritual of Flight."

Instinctively, Uriel and the other angel dragged Duma away from the door, clearing the space around Lucifer and Michael.

Lucifer took a step forward. Michael towered over him by three hands breadth.

"You are quite brave to set foot here," Michael said.

"Are you going to throw me out again?"

"I did not throw you out the first time."

"How soon they forget."

"So Light Giver, who oversees Hell in your absence? Sariel, Olivier, Azza, poor Etergus even?"

"Verrier."

Michael touched a small half circle scar under his eye. "I remember him."

"He sends his regards."

"I see."

"I, Lucifer the Morning Star, would humbly seek an audience with the Lord."

"It would be best if you left," Michael said.

"Have the rules changed also?" Lucifer said. "I repeat. I seek an audience with the Lord."

"Leave lest I cut off your black wings and mount them in my aerie."

"Oh my. How proper. How arrogant. Once again, I hum—"

"Escort the prince out of the City and beyond the Field of Gold," Michael said to Uriel. "See that he enters the Darkness."

Neither angel moved. Duma scooted until his back was against the wall.

"Leave lest I cleave your black heart—" Michael interrupted his own speech with a movement to the hilt of his sword.

"Perhaps request is the wrong impression." Lucifer reached into his cloak and handed Michael a rolled piece of parchment. "I have been summoned."

Michael read it and shook his head in disbelief.

"In another painting," Lucifer said. "I would destroy you."

Michael's head tilted, puzzled, then his face flushed and his sword caught flame.

The guard angels gasped and cleared even further away from the two giants.

Lucifer took a quick step back and dropped to one knee. Straightened out his neck.

Michael raised his sword. Brought it down with celerity. The air filled with a whistling sound as a score of angels sharply drew in a breath.

A quarter of the way through the stroke the sword stopped, hovering in mid-air. Michael's eyes glazed over. The sword lowered and extinguished itself as Michael sheathed it. Maintaining the trance, he spoke, although the voice was not his.

"Light Giver?"

"Yes, Milord?"

"You require an audience?"

"Humbly."

"Follow Mika'il."

Michael led Lucifer through the Grand Hall toward the

back of the Spire and up the spiral staircase's thousand steps.

Neither flew.

They stopped at a small wooden door, fashioned of oak.

Michael stood at the door, blinked twice, his eyes sharp and narrow.

"We will meet again, Light Giver."

"Yes, I suppose we will," Lucifer said with a small amount of resignation in his voice. He reached into his robe and produced an ornate sheath decorated with a mosaic of events past, present and future. The dagger's hilt and handle were simple, yet elegant in design. He held it out level at arm's length. "It has not been drawn since the Fall."

Michael took it. "It will remain as it is," he said. "Until—"

"I trust it will be," Lucifer said.

The small door opened. Lucifer paused as though to say something and then entered the Presence.

FOUR: *THE BODY*

MAGGIE DREAMED of burning, of charred and cracked flesh. She dreamed of pain, and then awoke with a shout in the first time in her many years. Something was burning. The cigar thumped to the ground, dumping ashes onto the small rug. She picked up the small nub and extinguished it, feeling rather stupid and old for falling asleep with it lit.

She loved their smell and would sometimes fall asleep with the aroma fresh in her mind and would dream of Harry. She thought fondly of their fortieth wedding anniversary when they had actually shared a cigar given to them by her brother. Maggie found it odd that among the many years of their roller coaster marriage that this memory was so prevalent. She made a mental note to send her brother a letter soon.

Her hands ached, and she rubbed some ointment into them. She pulled on Harry's old field jacket. She'd heard a coyote sniffing around the cabin last night so she grabbed her shotgun and left for a walk in the morning light.

∞

She and her husband first met back when she was moonlighting at Alice's Diner and going to business school during the day, when they both had thick hair. She had him pegged for a bad boy, which even then she found annoying, but still alluring. Maggie had danced with a number of rich boys and had found them more often than not to be very boring, not what she wanted at all as a young girl. She also pegged Harold as a leg-man, the way he watched most girls walk by, which she did whenever she got the chance, turning on her best hip sway.

And when he finally approached her he smiled and said, "Want to go polish off a bottle with me, you Irish lass?"

"It's Maggie, and I'm not Irish."

"Not yet," he said with a wink.

She accepted against her better judgment. Although they never got around to the bottle, they did stay up drinking coffee at another diner around the corner. They both took it with cream and sugar.

She replayed the first date in her mind, pleasantly surprised at the faint ghost-throbbing between her legs. She touched her hand there for a moment, looking around foolishly like a schoolgirl might.

"Oh Harold McCreedy, you were a silver tongued devil."

She continued her walk on a dirt path in the wooded area, relishing the sharp chilly air and the crunching of fallen leaves beneath her feet. She'd continued on for a half mile more when a coughing spasm struck her. She stopped to pull a hanky out of her jacket pocket, and tried to take a slow deep breath to arrest the attack but the tickle in her throat would not subside. Finally, after a few long minutes it eased somewhat. The back of her throat throbbed and tears rolled down her face from the effort.

She inhaled slowly again, daring the cough to come back, and noticed a change in the air.

Burning leaves.

No, something else, she thought. It seemed to come from up ahead. She continued on her way, not a little alarmed at the thought of a fire, but the smell wasn't quite right.

As she rounded the bend she thought it was more akin to the smell of…

rotting wood?

Up ahead, two small trees lay across the path. The splintered yellow of the stumps contrasted with burnt bark. As she got closer she noticed more trees had also toppled along the path. Thin wispy smoke rose from the center among the leaves. She heard something rustle among the leaves, snorting.

Curiously, she edged forward.

A coyote paced back and forth on lanky legs, sniffing and pawing at something.

She fired her gun into the air.

It looked at her for the briefest of moments with yellow eyes and darted off deeper into the woods.

The smell grew stronger until finally she saw a black round object. She thought for a moment, no, it couldn't be, but there it was.

A charred body.

No.

Two bodies.

Which was a surprise in Maggie's book, but not as much of one compared to what happened next.

One of the bodies spoke.

FIVE: *THE QUEST*

THUNDER CRASHED within the hall. Again the angels shuddered, the younger ones fearing The End, the older ones awaiting the Sound of the Trumpet.

Again the thunder crashed.

"NO!" The thunder echoed again, shaking the Spire itself. A pane of glass cracked and fell silently through the air and shattered into bastard diamonds on the marble floor. One angel swooped down, oblivious to everything but the immediate duty of cleaning. Within seconds there was no trace of the pane's fall.

Michael stormed across the Grand Hall, tongues of flames licking from the hilt of his sword. Duma stared intently wondering what had just transpired. Michael turned to him, and Duma lowered his eyes, hoping not to catch his gaze. And then he was gone through the doors of the First Grand Spire.

Curious and not a little fearful, Duma climbed to his feet while the others remained motionless. He stepped gingerly to the door and chanced a glance outside down the streets of the Silver City. He scanned the curved road and then the sky, but saw no trace of Michael. What he did see was the sides of the street filled with angels, Sarim, Cherub, all orders and dominions. They lined the sides a hundred deep and all the way to the horizon.

The whole city's here.

And then the buzzing again. And the smell of rotting wood. He turned.

Lucifer smiled. "Greetings, Duma."

Duma's voice failed him. He gasped, choked once and then twice.

"How is your wing?"

"It is—"

"I heard about Cassiel's eye."

Just then one of the guard angels approached them, stopping closer to Duma rather than to Lucifer. "Does he know?"

Lucifer shook his head.

The angel went into a trance, and spoke in a voice not his. *"Duma. Escort the Morning Star past the Field of Gold to the Edge of the Southern Slope."*

"Me?"

The angel guard laughed. *"Yes, Little One."*

Duma swallowed hard. His nose wrinkled.

"I—"

But Lucifer had already taken off. Duma trailed behind him bounding down the stairs to the sidewalk, having to exert an effort to keep up on foot.

As they walked the buzz of conversation among the angels died and then picked up as though the unlikely pair emitted a sphere of silence. Duma could make out an occasional word here and there from behind and to the front of them as they headed for the edge of the Silver City. No one laughed or mocked the pair.

"A quiet town, is it not?" Lucifer said.

Duma gave a small shrug, not sure whether the Light Giver was jesting or not.

At the edge of the Silver City, Lucifer turned to Duma and asked, "Do you wish to walk or fly?"

Duma just stared at him.

"You are right," Lucifer said. "It is a good day to walk."

Duma nodded.

A contingent of angels took flight at the edge of the City, saw that the pair was not doing likewise and settled quietly back to the ground. As they approached the Field of Gold, Lucifer gestured to the land. "This used to be a forest. Before the Fall."

"I know," Duma said, instantly regretting the incidental tone in his voice.

Lucifer paused. "Of course you do, Duma. Forgive me."

They traveled in silence for several miles, and as they topped the last hill the Edge of the Southern Slope came into view. Duma could make out a figure standing less than two feet away from the Edge. It was Michael, his hair swirling and lifting upwards as the Winds of Darkness tried to sweep into Heaven.

Lucifer and Duma reached the Edge. Michael did not make eye contact with either one of them. Duma did not understand, but took a few steps back, his escorting done.

The population of the City joined around them in a semi-circle. The back of the crowd took flight and within a minute, they were surrounded by a living wall; hovering as if seated in a coliseum. Duma could not see the hills or the Field or the City any more.

Michael stood silently, one hand on his sword's hilt, the other holding Lucifer's sheathed dagger.

Lucifer turned to Duma with a smile. "Are you prepared?"

"Prepared? Prepared for what?"

"To fall."

"Fall? But I—"

"Duma," Michael said, his voice flat and neutral. "You are to escort the Light Giver—"

"Escort?"

"Yes," Lucifer said. "We are embarking on a quest."

"Where?"

"Tell him, Michael."

Flat and neutral still. "The mudball."

"Earth?"

"Oh yes," Lucifer said.

"I'm to escort you to earth..." Duma chewed on this for a moment. "And what is the object of our quest?"

"Tell him, Mika'il," Lucifer said, and then stepped into the swirling Darkness and disappeared.

The smell of rotting wood flared briefly, and then it too was gone.

Michael turned to Duma. "The Book of Life."

SIX: *THE FALL*

THEY

f

e

l

l

for nine days.

SEVEN: *THE SIGIL*

MAGGIE MCCREEDY DRAGGED the body down the path towards her cabin. Leaves crumbled as the body skidded over twigs and leaves and acorn shells, making random popping sounds like corn in hot oil.

The body had spoken to her. Some language she couldn't understand. At first she thought it might be a moan. It drew her closer, past what she might have considered a safe distance, but she was not afraid. And the voice became melodic, pure and soothing. The sense of serenity seemed to grow stronger the closer she got. She kneeled beside it.

Its blackened hand moved towards her.

Help me.

Did she actually hear that? Her hand moved towards it

and stopped just shy. She stood up, deciding on another course of action, and took off her jacket.

"Let's get you out of this neck of the woods."

She stopped to catch her breath for a moment, easing on the tension in the jacket. It was a poor litter, but she hardly felt like finding two suitable branches long enough.

A sharp pain in her chest squeezed the breath out of her, and she sat down on the dirt path beside the body. She waited a minute and the pain passed. "Getting old, lassie."

She thought of Sapphire and her reaction to a situation like this.

Probably shit her bloomers.

She leaned closer to the body, and again felt a sense of tranquility. And there was something else. The pungent smell of burnt flowers— was it?— tweaked her nose. Huge patches of charred skin on the legs and feet had flaked off like dead bark, revealing a pinkish newborn skin.

She tentatively reached out and picked up a piece of the old skin. It felt like bark, coarse and crunchy. She pulverized a piece of it with little effort, and the smell grew even stronger. She gathered a few pieces and placed them in her jacket and marveled at her calmness.

I should be stroking out.

And then she thought of the old hidden camera show where the lady wheels a car into the garage. The mechanic opens the hood to see that there is no motor, and he just stands there with a blank expression on his face because his brain is telling him that this is not what should be there.

"Well, stranger. Am I supposed to take you home and feed you or take some steel wool to your skin and clean you up a little?"

The stranger did not answer.

"I thought as much."

Maggie knelt beside him. She gathered a handful of acorn shells and wrapped them in her handkerchief and started to gently scrub off some of the larger areas of dead flesh. After several minutes, she'd cleaned most of the body.

Satisfied, she spit in both hands and rubbed then together and started pulling the litter down the path.

"Well, stranger. You better end up being grist for the mill or I'm going to be very disappointed."

An hour and several stops later, Maggie reached the cabin.

She stood and looked back and forth between the barn and the cabin. Finally, she decided she was old enough to take some chances. She did have the shotgun, after all.

∞

Maggie McCreedy collapsed on the floor, panting for breath.

"Christ, you are a heavy one."

She'd tried for almost half an hour to get him onto the bed. She referred to "it" as a him although, apparently, the sex was indeterminate. As she was preparing to roll the body onto its back, she noticed a scar on the back of its neck. Upon closer inspection she realized it was a brand.

Maggie picked up one of the several notepads scattered about the cabin and drew a quick sketch of the brand. She rolled him over onto his back. Small pieces of blackened skin littered the bed sheets like crumbs.

She stared at him for a moment and thought she might have seen movement under the eyelids. She continued to stare and saw nothing.

A sudden chill shook through her body dispelling the sense of calmness she'd felt earlier. With a groan, she plucked a cowbell down from the wall and set it gently on the stranger's chest.

She left the room and shut the door. It had no lock so she tucked a chair under the knob and wedged the doorstop under it with a couple of labored kicks. And then she loaded up her shotgun and went after the other body.

∞

The next finger of scotch burned going down putting her, as far as Maggie McCreedy could tell, two shakes of a squirrel's tale from being drunk. She set the glass down on the wooden deck and rocked back and forth on her porch swing, the shotgun cradled in her arm like a surrogate grandbaby.

The other body had disappeared. And she was trying not to think of the one in the house.

Lawdy, lawdy, Ms. Clawdy.

Howlin' Wolf's gravelly gasoline voice quieted. The needle on her turntable bumped and hissed its end rhythm. She got up from the porch swing, stepped off the porch and squeezed off two rounds.

Thirty yards away, slugs shredded stacks of Sapphire romance novels.

"Ashes to ashes, pulp to pulp, you little wench."

She staggered out to the stacks and scattered the demolished white pages and painted covers of well-endowed couples with a swift kick. In the center of the debris, she dropped her stack of legal yellow pads containing the new Sapphire book. She took off the cap to a fat red marker with her teeth and drew a big circle on the top page and then a big dot in the center, circling it over and over until the ink soaked through and tore the page.

Maggie took a step back and looked at her handiwork. She nodded satisfaction to herself and felt the trees sway unnaturally to her left and then right.

She backed up, almost tripping on dirt. Then sighting the manuscript down the length of the shotgun, she jerked the trigger.

Next thing she knew she was in pain. Her hip. The recoil had knocked her drunken ass to the ground. The manuscript mocked her with its two red eyes.

Shoot the one in the middle.

She winced at the pain and somewhere far away thought, that's going to hurt when I sober up.

She targeted the stack again. And this time *squeezed* the trigger.

Hit.

Autumn exploded, and all the leaves were yellow and covered in her handwriting.

She loaded another shell, and then she heard it.

The muted thudding of the cowbell.

EIGHT: *THE ARTIST*

A CIRCLE BURNED itself into the earth, and two creatures materialized within its perimeter.

"The Book of Life is missing?" Duma said, alarmed. "Who could have the Book— but that would mean—"

"We will do well on our journey if you refrain from asking questions more than once," Lucifer said, stepping out of the circle filled with purpose. "But I do appreciate your enthusiasm. I always have."

"But I do not understand. Why are you looking for the Book of Life, why not Mika'il or Ramiel?"

Lucifer leapt over a small brook. A tiny fish jumped from it and Lucifer snatched it out of the air. "They would not want to dirty their feet."

Duma took two steps to Lucifer's one and stepped on

stones to cross. "Their legs would get tired," he said. "They are lazy, flying everywhere. No adventure in that."

"May I remind you that this is not an adventure—"

"A quest then."

"A means to an end," Lucifer said and let the fish slide from his hand back to its watery home.

Duma watched the fish swim away. Then he scanned the surrounding area. "Is the Book out here somewhere?"

"No, but there is a small town over that hill. And in that town, a man."

∞

That man sat holding his head in his hands, sobbing. Random streaks of light shot through tears in the tin foil covering the windows. Static dominated a college basketball game playing silently on the TV behind him. His hair was unkempt from constant finger-combing. Patches of a beard shadowed his face. Red nicks, fresh and old lined his chin like errant pen marks. An antique Colt Peacemaker pistol in well kept condition lay at his side on a cot, uncocked.

A number of unfinished canvases lined the dilapidated apartment on homemade easels: Charcoals, pastels, oils, and watercolors; variations on Doré, Gustave Moreau and the like. *The Fall of Man, The Fall of Lucifer, Salome Dancing Before Herod, Jacob and the Angel*; punishment, retribution, redemption. None finished.

He took a heavy drag on a paint-stained cigarette and tore off the seal to a bottle of vodka. It took him all of a minute to kill it. Then he picked up the phone and dialed a number from a business card.

What followed was a slow deliberate conversation in which the man grew more and more angry. Finally, he simply unplugged the phone, popped open the cylinder on the revolver and slid home a single shell.

A bang sounded.

The man looked up. He'd nailed two by fours across the doorjamb several days ago. He waited, sucking on the cigarette, feeling the burning gravel at the back of his throat.

He spun the cylinder, watching it like a roulette wheel. And then with great care filled it with hollow point bullets.

From the shadows of a larger painting, Lucifer showed himself. "Greetings, Victor."

Victor just sat there and then raised the gun with great effort. "No more." Desperation laced his voice.

"No more of what?" Lucifer said.

"Of you," Victor said.

"Do you know who I am?"

"One of them." His tired eyes flicked from painting to painting. "Them."

"Not just one of them," Lucifer said, sounding slightly

offended. Egos are such delicate things.

"Get out of my head," Victor said. The gun drooped in his hands. "Get the fuck out of my head."

Lucifer could see now that Victor's eyes were completely red from hemorrhaging. Half moons of lividity hung under his eyes.

"I am here, Victor," Lucifer said. "Not in your head. Here in this room."

Hands trembling, Victor brought the gun up again.

Lucifer gracefully moved to a chair stacked high with paintings. He removed them and set them gently on the floor and took a seat.

"They won't go away," Victor said. A bloody tear rolled down his cheek.

"How long have they been with you?"

"Make them stop." He put the gun to his head. "Or I will."

Lucifer sighed.

Duma emerged from the shadows.

"I know you," Victor said. "Both of you. Yes, you've been there sometimes."

"In your visions?"

He nodded.

"Now you've come for me?"

"No," Duma said. "What do you think is happening to you?"

"I'm going mad."

"No, Victor, you are quite sane although you may be feeling the contrary."

"What's happening to me? I've tried everything." He motioned to his nightstand. A kaleidoscope of pills lay scattered and useless next to a dozen empty Visine bottles. "I quit sleeping."

"How long?"

"I haven't slept in a month."

Lucifer considered this. "In your visions have you seen a book?"

"A book?"

"It's a very special book, Victor, more important than any book in Creation."

"I don't know, so many things, I've seen." The gun fell to his lap. "They're all just dreams, right? Or am I seeing something, about to happen, or what has... I don't understand."

Duma looked at some photos from years ago housed in cracked frames. "You've been a priest for sometime."

"Yes."

"So therefore you believe in the Scriptures," Lucifer said. "In the angels."

There was a slight hesitation, "yes."

"Demons and devils."

More hesitation.

"*Yetzer hara,*" Lucifer said. "The evil is within us."

"Victor, you are being subjected to channeling from an angel," Duma said. "You are being sent the visions. They are *not* being manufactured by your brain."

"Who is doing this to me?" Red ran from his eyes. "I've lived my life without sin, for the most part, I've been loyal, I've kept... the faith." The gun fell to the floor.

Duma and Lucifer let him weep for a few minutes. And then he looked up. "Yes, I see now," Victor said. "The Lord has sent you to test me."

"No, there is no test."

"Yes," Victor said, stemming the flow of tears with a paint spotted sleeve. "You seek the Book of Life." He blinked. "For your own purposes."

"I am seeking it for the Lord, Victor. And while that may seem like an impossibility--"

"Lord of Lies..."

"Victor. I have been instructed to destroy those that stand in the Presence's way. Do you understand that? By standing in my way, you are standing in the Presence's way. Hell will await you, and I can assure you an eternity is just a bit longer than you might think."

"I can't accept what you are saying as the truth," Victor said, digging his ragged fingernails into his cheeks. "How could I?"

Duma and Lucifer exchanged glances.

"We should get used to this kind of nonsense," Lucifer said.

Duma spoke. "There are two angels, Sopheriel Memeth and Sopheriel Mehayye, twins, if you will, who watch over the Books of Life and Death. The twins, as well as the Book of Life, are missing. Lucifer has been charged with finding the missing book."

"God make a deal with the devil?" He shook his head. *"No."*

"You are being fed visions by one of the twin angels," Lucifer said. "I require that knowledge of the Book. What particular visions have you received?"

Victor picked up a thick Bible and held it. "In the name of Christ, I rebuke you."

Duma and Lucifer looked at each other. Lucifer rose. He took the Bible from Victor's bloody hands and threw it to Duma.

"Little man, the Presence has empowered me to destroy you for what you are doing. Your faith and loyalty are to be admired, but as you were once so fond of saying 'you are preaching to the choir.'"

"May God forgive me." Victor picked up the revolver, but Lucifer snatched his hand, crushing the bones.

Victor screamed.

"I will ask you but one more time—"

"Lucifer…" Duma said.

"Silence, Little One." He turned to Victor and released his hand. Splinters of bone protruded from Victor's hand like white spines on a red cactus. The gun slipped from useless fingers.

Victor closed his eyes and began praying in a whisper and then said, "Damn you."

"You will not ever mock me again, Victor." And then hooking a clawed finger, Lucifer ripped out Victor's throat.

Arterial spray misted the room, adding a scarlet touch of abstraction to several pieces of canvas. Duma knelt down and held Victor's hand as he gasped and wheezed through the gash in his neck.

Lucifer stood over the body watching the death throes.

"I cannot believe I once considered joining the Fall," Duma whispered.

"It was what I was instructed to do," Lucifer said. "That was made clear."

Victor quit moving. A red bubble formed on his throat and then popped. Nothing more.

Duma took the soiled sheet from Victor's bed and placed it on the chair and then picked up Victor and placed him on the bed. He covered the body with a dirty sheet.

"*Alevasholem.*"

Lucifer watched silently.

Then Duma took another Bible from the shelves and laid it on Victor's chest, nestling the first one they had taken from him in the crook of his wing.

"These paintings," Duma said. "Most are not of earth, but this one is of a lake. There is something washed up on its beach."

"That is our next location."

Duma did not answer him. But instead stood in silence staring at the body of the priest. "Before we go, Morning Star, I would suggest we find one other thing."

"Yes?"

"A witness not of the Host."

NINE: *THE FOLD*

THEY LANDED on the uppermost branches able to bear their earthly weight. In the distance, a small ranch house and weathered barn.

Duma rubbed the top of his shoulders wincing with the effort.

"Would you like me to rub those?"

"No."

"How long has it been since you took flight, Little One?"

"Before your arrival in the City, not since I battled Cassiel."

"A long time for an angel not to fly. You've been walking longer than some humans have had family trees."

Lucifer touched both his hands to Duma's shoulders.

"Do not," Duma said and then stopped his protest. His shoulders burned for a moment as a great heat flared and then died. The pain as well as the soreness disappeared.

"Let us recruit our witness."

∞

Maggie looked through the peephole. Set her bottle of Jim Bean down and opened the door, shotgun raised to thigh level. She saw a tall fellow and a somewhat shorter fellow.

"You folks aren't peddling the *Watchtower,* are you?"

Neither said anything for a long moment.

"My associate and I require your services," the short one finally said. "We wish to commission a piece of writing, or documentation rather."

"Yeah, well, everyone thinks their life story is worth telling," Maggie said. "I tell you what, I'll give you the address and number of my agent, and she'll—"

"Maggie," the tall one said. "There is no percentage for you to split with your agent."

"If it don't make dollar, fellas, it don't make sense."

"If we may come in for a moment," the shorter one said in a non-threatening tone.

She considered it for a second and noticed the tall one's eyes were much like her husband's. She motioned them in with the gun.

They took a seat and then the smaller one sneezed. He picked up something from the floor. The bigger one paid him no mind, but continued to look at Maggie.

"Listen very carefully to what we are going to say," he said.

∞

"So the Book of Life is a register of God's faithful," Maggie said.

"Yes, those people will be introduced to the Hosts of Heaven at the time of Revelation," Duma said.

"Something I would have thought you," she said, indicating Lucifer. "Would be interested in stopping."

"No," Lucifer said, simply.

"If I was sober," Maggie said. "I'd probably shoot you both. But you're not the first weird thing to happen to me today, and I happen to find you entertaining as hell. No pun intended."

Duma snickered and drew a look of disapproval from Lucifer.

"Why a human writer?" Maggie said, smirking.

He ran his long fingers through his hair, changing its color to chestnut.

Maggie suddenly had the urge to run her fingers through his hair like she'd have done to Harold. Puzzled, she shook off the feeling.

"Many tales have passed the lips of storytellers," Lucifer said. "Many books gather dust on neglected shelves. All these tales, all these testaments. The Fallen, the rebel, the eater of children, et cetera. But this tale, our journey into mystery, I wish documented by a witness, first hand testimony written in a timely manner, not years later, like those Books."

"Why this particular story?" Maggie said, not liking the fact she was starting to sober.

"That, Maggie McCreedy, will be your mystery," Lucifer said.

"I've got a question," Maggie said.

"Please," Lucifer said.

"Explain the dinosaurs and why they aren't in the Bible."

"That is your question?"

"Yeah, smart guy."

"I will humor you, Maggie. The dinosaurs are mentioned in the Bible. In Exodus, and I quote the original Hebrew translation, Moses' staff is thrice turned into a snake, but this animal is called a *nahash* the first time, a *taneen* the second and a *nahash* the third time. *Nahash* is the Hebrew word for snake. We know that from its use the first time that it must still mean snake the third time. But the word *taneen* denotes a general category of animals. That word appears in the creation chapter of Genesis, where other than Adam, only general categories of life are listed. Therefore *taneen* must be the general category within which *nahash*, or snake, falls. The general category for snakes is reptile. Thus Genesis 1:21 translates as: 'And God created the big reptiles.' The biggest reptiles were the dinosaurs."

"Why doesn't it specify the dinosaurs directly?"

"That is inconsistent with the pattern of the chapter. The entire account of Genesis is stated in terms of objects known or knowable to the myriad of witnesses present at Sinai 3,300 years ago. But it is hinted at."

Maggie chewed on that for a minute. "I guess I need to get me a new Bible. Hebrew, huh?" She cleaned her glasses with her hanky. "What about God creating everything in six days. How was that possible?"

"Time is non-existent," Duma said. "Light operates outside of time. At the point of the Creation there was no earth perspective for a day, nor even light, for that matter was not created until the third day. Quite simply put—"

Lucifer cleared his throat. "I think, Little One, that Maggie would prefer a miracle instead of an explanation." He smiled. "Besides, time is of the essence."

"I still don't know," Maggie said. "I—"

"How is your vision?"

"My eyes," Maggie said. "They're not quite as sharp."

Suddenly, Lucifer was in front of her. He touched the

sides of her head.

"Dear Lord," she said and took her glasses off.

Everything was as sharp, no sharper, than when she was a little girl. She also found she was completely sober. "A miracle." She paused. "But I don't want to be beholden... to you."

Lucifer cocked his head. "Beholden to me," he said thoughtfully.

Maggie straightened her flannel shirt, buying a moment to regain her composure. "I don't think that's fair play. That is if I were to be your witness to your journey I don't think it would be fair of me to accept any favor or the such."

"Perhaps afterward," Duma suggested.

"So be it," Lucifer said. He touched her temples.

Her world turned blurry and enlarged as it went out of focus to the point of making her legally blind.

"Shall we?"

Her glasses slipped to the end of her nose. She adjusted them, not cursing them as was her normal reaction. Then again, it hadn't been a normal day.

She offered them some clothes from Harry's closet. She'd never planned to throw them out. As they finished dressing themselves she gave them a bit of news.

"I had another couple of visitors today."

"Two of them?"

"Smelled a hell of a lot like you. Found them all crispy down a patch of trail. One of them was still alive."

Her visitors were taken off guard.

"I can see that this interests you," she said to Lucifer. She turned to Duma. "You look a little spooked also."

She picked up her notepad and flipped to the sketch she'd made earlier. Held it up.

Duma gasped. "Seems we've got a winner,"

Maggie said, and slapped her thigh.

Neither of the strangers joined in her mirth.

She downed another shot and told them about her encounter. "Duma here picked up a bit of one of their skins off the floor. Thought I'd swept it all up."

Duma looked pensive.

Lucifer held out his hand.

Duma placed a bark-like piece gently in his hand.

He crumbed it and then smelled it. And suddenly he grew pensive also.

"I brought him here," Maggie said. "But he soon hightailed it out the window."

Rocking back and forth, Duma ran his fingers over his recently acquired Bible. "Is it him?"

"It means nothing," Lucifer said.

"He's here." Duma continued to rock. "And he's not alone."

"Who are we talking about?" Maggie said, sharpening a

pencil.

"He came without Blessing," Lucifer said. "That would explain his condition."

"But that would mean—" Duma started.

"Fetch your pencil, pad, and coat, writer," Lucifer said. He etched a circle in the wooden floor with the edge of his wing.

Maggie did as she was told, while Duma drew symbols in the air.

"What are you doing?"

He guided her inside the circumference of the roughly etched circle. "We are going to a lake."

"Who are you talking about?"

"He Who is as God." Duma finished his air tracings and the trio disappeared.

TEN: *HONEYBONE*

"ANDREW?"

Water lapped the edges of the shore washing over the flesh-stripped toes of the bloated corpse.

"Andy?" Lucifer stroked its hair. "Andy Honeybone?"

Some indeterminable weeds intertwined with the hair of the pale body. Green and purple veins zigzagged here and there like underground highways beneath the translucent flesh.

The eyelids were partially gone. Maggie could almost see the pupils. Foam leaked from the lipless mouth, the soft tissue having been eaten away by scavengers. An expensive sailing shirt stretched tight across its alabaster torso and arms.

"Andrew Honeybone?"

What was left of the eyelids pulled back. The eyes pulled in narrow and came to focus. "Yes," the corpse said, and then its bloated arms doubled over its bulbous stomach. "I dreamed I was in Heaven, I think it was. It was kind of gray. What's happening?"

"You died."

"No, this is one of those dreams within a dream. Must have been that salmon," the corpse said. "I thought it smelled funny." He grabbed his stomach again. "It hurts."

Lucifer poked a hooked finger through the soft flesh of the corpse's belly.

Gas whooshed from it.

Maggie choked and her stomach knotted. She fanned her hand under her nose.

"Better?"

"Yes," the corpse said.

"You are Andrew Honeybone?" Lucifer said. "I'd hate to think I've awoken the wrong corpse."

"Yes, I'm Andrew Honeybone, attorney at law," the corpse wrinkled his nose. "Is that smell me?"

Lucifer nodded.

"How long have I been dead?"

"Since yesterday."

"Yesterday in my dream, right? I'm not really--"

"Not yet. You're still in Illinois."

"Still in hell, huh?" He laughed harshly. Water gushed from his mouth. "I guess I slipped from the *Grace*— that's my boat." He scanned the horizon over the water. "I don't see her." He paused for a moment. His eyes rolled in their sockets, lumpy and rough like poorly shelled hard-boiled eggs. He tried to stand and stumbled.

Lucifer helped him gain his balance and then wiped his hands on his jeans. "If you prefer to think this a dream then do so."

Maggie took a half step back, her arms crossed in front of her as though she were cold.

"I'm not normally this bloated," Andy said, with a smile full of sand. He felt the gash on his abdomen. "Nor am I likely to be again. I suppose."

"Let's get on with it," Lucifer said, and began up the sandy trail.

Maggie pulled out a yellow legal pad and began to scribble on it.

"Moody fellow, isn't he?" Honeybone said.

"I reckon." Maggie turned the page and jotted some more notes.

"What are you writing?" Andy said. "My obituary?"

"Mine," Maggie said.

Andy turned to Duma.

Duma shrugged and hurried to catch up with Lucifer. "What is this," Duma said. "How is he to aid us?"

"Hey, I was wondering," Honeybone said. "Could I maybe go and see my wife? She's pregnant with our first."

"She is not of our concern," Lucifer said.

Duma and Lucifer conversed in a foreign language. Maggie took notes on their gestures and tone.

"Damn lot of birds around here," Honeybone noted.

Maggie looked over her shoulder. Saw a flock of blackbirds flying overhead. Another landed in the trees behind them, filling the branches like dark pears.

"But he," indicating Honeybone, "was part of the vision," Duma said. "There must be a reason."

"To delay us, a trick perhaps."

The birds suddenly took flight as though spooked.

Duma and Lucifer looked up. "We would do well to leave."

"Yes, you are correct."

"What are you guys afraid of a flock of birds for?"

The angels quickened their pace.

Maggie watched them closely. Duma still holding the Bible to his chest, silently mouthing Scripture or prayer, or, it seemed to Maggie's fading hearing, a nursery rhyme. She did not understand the two of them often as a number of their exchanges were in languages foreign to her ears; sometimes they seemed to communicate without speaking at all.

Her joints ached, and the pain still throbbed in her hip.

She hawked up a load of the brown stuff and spat.

Duma seemed trepid about their journey; Lucifer focused and determined but with something akin to false arrogance. Duma stopped and drew a circle in the sand with his stronger wing.

She scribbled her thoughts, noting that the weather was overcast and gray. A purgatory of sorts.

The birds chirped and cawed, adding to the haunting afternoon. Duma stepped in the circle and traced ghost symbols in the air.

She looked at the walking corpse.

It could be worse.

Andrew Honeybone might have been a good-looking man now, but his cadaverous appearance was quite shocking.

"Does anyone have a mirror?" Honeybone asked. "I'd like to take a look at the smell."

∞

They each took a bale of hay in Maggie's barn and used them for a seat. Honeybone facing Duma and Lucifer.

"I don't get it."

"Neither do we," Duma said somewhat sympathetically. "Something has been taken from Heaven-- something very precious-- and we have been charged with its return."

"What was your name?" Honeybone said, poking some straw into his belly wound.

"Duma."

"Duma? That mean anything?"

"The quiet one."

"Hmmm," Honeybone pondered thoughtfully. "Okay, next question, why me?"

"You and your body of water were depicted quite clearly in a painting."

"By whom?"

"A priest."

"Ex-priest."

"And that's how you found me?"

"Yes, but the thing is we do not know what purpose you serve."

"If any."

"Why would a painting have any significance?"

"The priest was tortured with visions," Lucifer said. "He thought by painting them they would leave his head."

"Have you had any visions or odd dreams lately?" Duma said.

"Other than this dream here," Honeybone said, sarcastically. "I had a vision of air bubbling and rushing above me and a vision of darkness. Reminds me of a joke. What do you call 10,000 lawyers at the bottom of Lake

Michigan?"

Lucifer dismissed the punch line with a wave of his hand. "A book. Now think carefully. Have you any knowledge, vision or possession of a book?"

"I have several books," Honeybone said. "Describe it."

"An antique book, papyrus pages, lamb skin cover, silver stitching of angel's breath."

"Doesn't ring a bell."

A guttural growl rose up from Lucifer's throat. Birds in the rafters, took flight as though their roosts were on fire.

Honeybone shifted. "Do you know who took the book, I mean you guys have to have some kind of police or something," he said. "Do you have any suspects?"

"Creatures not of this earth, Mr. Honeybone," Lucifer said.

"That may not entirely be true," Duma muttered.

Lucifer shot him a glance. Maggie caught it. Thought of the two charred bodies. The one that spoke. She said nothing.

"My wife has strange dreams, but she's been having them for a while. She's nine months pregnant." Honeybone lowered his head and exhaled useless lungs slowly. "I'd like to see her. Is that possible?" He looked from Duma to Lucifer to Maggie waiting for an answer. "I mean not like this, but from a distance."

"We have more pressing matters," Lucifer said.

The birds flittered and reclaimed their roost.

"That priest," Honeybone said. "Why isn't he here?"

"He would not cooperate," Lucifer said.

Duma flipped through the Bible. Something slipped from it onto the dirt floor. The Little One picked it up. It was a small gold cross and chain. "The chain is broken." He turned the cross over, held it closer to face. "There's an inscription--"

"Ego te absolvo," Maggie said, focusing past Duma.

"Yes, how did you know?"

"Read the inside cover to the Bible."

Duma turned the book over quickly in his hands. *"To my little brother, Vic. This is for that one Sunday picnic twenty years ago. I love you, Mag."*

"Victor," Lucifer said. "Was your brother."

Maggie cast a questioning look at Lucifer. "Was?"

Silence.

"What happened to him?" Maggie said. "Did you kill Victor?"

"I put him to rest, Maggie McCreedy," Morning Star said. "He is no longer a tortured soul."

"You killed him."

"I neither relish nor enjoy this task." He stood and turned, arms and wings extended. "Touching the dirt with my feet, conversing with the likes of you, Maggie McCreedy. Or Honeybone. I do that which is commanded of me. And part of that was to destroy those that would stand in my way."

Maggie pulled out her lighter, flicked it with her thumb and held the dancing flame to the corner of a legal pad. "Fine by me."

The flame licked and waved, and the yellow pages darkened to brown, then black and caught fire.

"*No,*" Lucifer commanded.

Suddenly, a gust of wind blew through the barn extinguishing the burning papers and scattering them in the process. Duma scurried to pat out a few glowing embers. Ash and embers spiraled up like fireflies to the rafters as the gust died down.

"Don't you see, Shorty?" He called her by a nickname only Harold and Victor had ever used. "None of us have a choice in this." He waved his hand.

Tentatively, Duma approached her with a cluttered handful of papers extended toward her. "This story is your heart's desire," he said. "The story must be told, Maggie McCreedy."

"Not by me," she said, and spit in his eye.

ELEVEN: *NO FURY*

DUMA CHASED after her.

Maggie headed for her ranch house.

"This is not wise, Maggie. He is—"

Maggie whirled, her hip protesting the action. "Did he have to die?"

"The instructions," Duma said.

"Did my little brother have to die?"

"Your brother was steadfast in his convictions, if not his faith—"

"Did my brother have to die?" Maggie said. Her chest hitched. Something tightened.

Duma looked away, and Maggie stormed into the house. Gathered her shotgun and a handful of shells, ratcheting one home as she stepped back out onto the porch.

Honeybone wandered out of the barn. Lucifer followed.

"Uh-oh," Honeybone said and took a few quick sidesteps away from Lucifer.

"Maggie," was all Lucifer got out before the first round caught him in the upper right arm, tearing away a softball sized piece of meat and flesh.

Ratchet.

BLAM.

The second round caught him square in the chest. The third in the abdomen. Black liquid and pieces of internal organs spilled from his wound.

She struggled to ratchet the shotgun a fourth time. Her hands ached and cramped on her as she continued her advance. Her eyes burned from the smoke.

Lucifer staggered forward.

Please, one more.

She willed her gnarled hands to work.

And they did.

BLAM.

The fourth round took off the side of Lucifer Morning Star's face. He approached her wordlessly until the smoking barrel of her shotgun rested against his chest.

Somehow she found the strength to ratchet the gun yet another time. But found she was out of shells.

Lucifer slowly pushed the barrel aside. "You remind me of Lilith. Her spirit." He bent forward and kissed her softly on the forehead.

The gun fell to the ground. Maggie's knees gave way, and she collapsed at Lucifer's feet and sobbed quietly.

The birds seemed to cry with her.

Maggie pounded on his feet, grabbing bits of dirt and grass and flinging it at him.

He cupped her chin, wet with the flow of tears, and tilted her head up, exposing her neck.

He raised a clawed finger.

Birds screamed.

"For an eternity, Maggie McCreedy."

Maggie whispered, "The Lord is my shepherd I shall not want."

A raven landed on Lucifer's arm. Stabbed its beak into his flesh.

Lucifer shook its annoying grip loose. But then another landed on his shoulder. Stabbed at his face and then another and another.

More commotion. Dozens of ravens appeared and started pecking and scratching and fluttering in a flurry of feathers. The noise of the birds reached such a peak that Maggie opened her eyes and quickly backpedaled away from the now hundreds of birds that circled about Lucifer's body. Screaming, the black bodies dove at him in turns.

"Enough," Lucifer shouted and grabbed a bird from the air by its wing. Strips of twisted, jagged flesh hung from his hands.

Enraged, he dug his claws into the bird's body, crushing its chest.

A strong floral smell hit Maggie.

Lilacs...

Lucifer threw the raven's body to the ground. The birds retreated in perfect unison, whirling and twirling about forming one mass of black frenzied motion. And then the motion took shape. A man. He stepped forward. Only a few birds remained, and they took flight landing on the uppermost branches of the surrounding trees.

The form blurred and then came into sharp focus: A man with blue eyes and bright pink flesh, his head crowned with a thin fuzz of gold. And although he was sexless and ageless, the very sight of him took Maggie's breath away, and she found herself weeping again, not now at the death of her brother, but by the pure beauty of the creature.

She did not notice it holding its forearm. The corner of its eye twitched in what one might recognize as a grimace of pain.

Duma fell to a knee.

Honeybone wept.

The creature stood fully erect and stretched forth its wings like great sails.

Lucifer took a step back, trying to hold in his guts.

"Greetings, brother," the creature said.

"Greetings, Mika'il."

"He is as God," Duma whispered to himself.

Michael favored his shoulder, but managed a smile that made Maggie cringe. She retreated as nonthreateningly as she could in the face of two titans about to clash.

"So what is it this time, brother?" Lucifer said. "Jealousy?" He paused for the briefest second. "Again."

"You are still pathetic."

"I do not care."

"And when you fail in your quest," Michael said. "Do you expect that the Gates of Hell will still be open to you?"

Lucifer put a bloody hand on the hilt of his dagger. "I still have the key."

"Twice you will have betrayed your kind," Michael said. "I have heard stories already from the Seventh Circle. Have you?"

Lucifer shook his head, cradling his guts. Slowly, almost thoughtfully, he pushed them back in.

"And Duma, the Little Rebel. Still on the fringe, eh? At least your brother made a choice."

Duma stood, arched his wings, although the left one did not quite extend fully.

"Gotten some exercise for those finally. Good. Good."

"Michael, the Lord will be disappointed."

"Your words are tiny daggers, Little Rebel. Sharp, but pointless. Like your quest. A noble one, no? Mere folly for the Lord to see the Prince of the World running about witless. You see, Lucifer, you are a joke. They are laughing about you. In Heaven, in Hell and now on earth."

"You have had your good laugh. Besides, I am here with Blessing. You are not. How did it feel to burn with the cold as you fell for nine days?"

"Where will you go, O Fallen One? No entry into Hell, Heaven. Where on Earth will you go?"

"Hell is still mine, Michael."

"Perhaps you will revisit Eden," Michael said. "It is gray now. It would suit you."

Lucifer lifted his head and his arms dropped to his sides.

Maggie could see now that most of his wounds had closed, though parts of his face were still missing and his sharp teeth were visible through a gash in his cheek.

"It will be a small death," Michael said. "Sad and lonely and small."

"Michael, your words are full of pride and yet you see I will not fight you. For if I were to engage you there would indeed be a small and melancholy death. And the Fallen would celebrate, perhaps by releasing the tortured souls. Have you thought about that, Angel of Vengeance? Your death might well free the damned, but certainly the Fallen will drink from the tears of the Host."

And then a stone struck Michael between the eyes. He let out a yelp more of surprise than pain. A line of red ran down the bridge of his nose and divided like a stream against a rock.

"How is that for a choice?" Duma said, gathering another rock. "David would be proud, yes?"

Michael moved with a speed that defied physics. Duma leapt into awkward flight to escape, but was caught by the leg and hurled to the ground. Michael stood over the wounded Duma like a vulture.

"Leave only footprints, Little Rebel."

Michael reached down and in turn broke each of Duma's wings.

Duma howled with agony as twisted angel bone ground to powder. Michael then tore a handful of Duma's pinfeathers from his flesh as a huntsman's trophy. "Do not hurt the woman, Morning Star."

Michael leapt into the air and suddenly hundreds of ravens filled the sky.

Duma cursed. "I will destroy him."

Although there was much anger in his statement, there was little conviction, Maggie noticed. She climbed to her feet, hip flaring with pain.

Lucifer walked over to Duma and reached out to touch

his wings. Duma shied away and scampered to the barn on all fours like an animal, the look in his eyes quite clear.

"You did nothing to protect him," Maggie said.

Lucifer said nothing, touching his cheek and the teeth exposed behind it. He looked to Maggie and then the sky and headed for the barn. When he got to the door, he stopped and spun on his heel. Eyes narrowed as he scanned the area. His nostrils flared. Jaw muscles bulged.

"Where's Honeybone?"

TWELVE: *HONEYBONE'S TRAIL*

"WHERE IS HONEYBONE?" Lucifer screamed. The woods quieted. Even the wind dwindled to nothing.

"Why don't you scatter into a thousand birds and fly overhead and find him," Maggie said.

"It's not that easy," Lucifer said.

"It never is," Maggie said. "Is it?"

Lucifer pointed a finger at her. "You do not realize how blessed you are at this moment, Maggie McCreedy."

"Can you bring him back?" she said.

"Who?" Duma said, licking his wounds.

"My brother."

"That I cannot do," Lucifer said.

"You say that," Maggie said, "but you got Honeybone up and walking and talking after he drowned."

"Have you noticed the smell? Have you noticed the rot? He is not alive in the sense you are talking of."

Maggie kicked at some dirt, one of the spent shells from her gun.

"We have to find Honeybone," Lucifer said. "He may be an integral part of this puzzle."

Maggie yawned.

"Which way would be the easiest to travel on foot out of here?"

"The main road up to the gate, or there's a trail leading down yonder. Runs into the fence on the property line, but after that there's a highway. He'd be easier to spot than roadkill."

"Let's go."

Maggie shuffled her feet.

"Your brother is dead by my hand. Maggie, accept that and do the job you have agreed to do. We had a deal and you must realize the implications of breaking such a deal. I do not want your friendship, nor your forgiveness, but I need you as a witness. Grab your pad and pen, scribe. Let us find Honeybone before the world finds him."

∞

"Does it hurt?" Maggie asked Duma.

Duma's wings were folded loosely against his back at

unnatural angles. "Quite."

The pair walked in silence, Maggie scribbling on her pad. Lucifer, up ahead, walked quickly.

"What's it like?"

"Playing escort to the Prince of the World? He's rather boring after awhile— in an unpredictable way. I have not seen him since the Fall, when I almost joined them."

"Why didn't you?"

He shrugged and winced. "This place is not so different from Heaven."

"My husband and me lived here. He passed away last summer. We built this ranch ourselves. He was quite good with his hands."

Duma smiled.

She smiled back. "Victor had been meaning to come visit here. Been saying that for a quite a few summers. Poor son of a bitch."

"For what it is worth," Duma said. "He was brave to the end. He did not go quietly, like most. For what it is worth."

"Not the salt in my tears."

Duma nodded as if understanding.

A minute passed. Duma stretched the lower part of his wings out. "Mika'il." He spit on the ground. "Lucifer should have slain him then. I would have…"

"Really?"

"Perhaps." Duma kicked a stone. It bounced down the trail, hit a divot and took a long tall hop, thudding against the back of Lucifer's leg. He turned sharply, but said nothing.

"I dare say he's shown great restraint. Not so much with your brother, or even you, but with the Host." He turned his head upwards. Nostrils flared. "Something is definitely in the air."

Maggie scribbled some more. "How long will it take for your wings to mend?"

Duma shrugged with a grimace. "They may not. It's like that sometimes. Our bodies."

"I'm sorry," Maggie said sincerely.

He shrugged again. "I prefer to walk."

∞

Lucifer stopped and bent down.

They joined him.

"What is it?"

Lucifer picked up a piece of cloth and a feather.

Duma sighed.

Maggie leaned over to Duma. "What is that?"

"Part of Honeybone's ear," Lucifer said, squeezing the ear into a fleshy blob. "And a feather."

"I don't get it," Maggie said.

"It appears that Michael has either destroyed dear Mr. Honeybone," Duma said. "Or kidnapped him."

Hate and contempt swirled around Lucifer's slit irises.

"Do you think he killed Honeybone?"

"No," Lucifer said. "Mika'il has him."

"How can you be certain?"

"Because he would rather possess something I want than destroy it."

"Where'd he take him?" Maggie asked. "Heaven?"

"Oh, no. They wouldn't allow him in toting a load such as Mr. Honeybone," Duma said.

"I don't know what they would let into Heaven anymore, Little One," Lucifer said. "But he is not there, I can be fairly certain of that."

"And I would venture that he would not go to—" Duma cleared his throat. "Hell."

"Not without my head on a pike and a legion behind him."

"I doubt he would need the legion," Duma said.

"So you still respect him after the great display of battle prowess with your wings," Morning Star said. "You disappoint me, Little One."

Duma turned away from Lucifer, head hung low. He muttered something under his breath. Bent down and picked up a rock, turned it over in his hand. He stared at it for a long second as though gazing into a crystal ball and then slid the stone into his pocket. "Methinks Michael knows more about this than his demeanor may have suggested."

"If he followed us here and Maggie did in fact nurse Michael back to health," Lucifer said with some disgust.

"He did stop you from killing me," Maggie said. "I guess that makes him and me even." She scribbled something as though marking a scorecard.

Lucifer dismissed her words with a flippant wave of his hand. "If he was charred— and we have seen a piece of his flesh— then he did not come to Earth with Blessing, but on his own; a rogue if you will. He will not be so quick to return to Heaven. Unless he has the Book. And the key to that, at the moment, seems to be Mr. Honeybone."

"You should have killed Michael," Duma said. "Pretentious little--"

"Watch your tongue, Little One. I will not back your words."

Duma grumbled.

"I suppose we better step up the business of finding Honeybone," Maggie said.

"I suggest we go back," Duma said, sitting off to the side. "And examine more paintings."

"Paintings?"

"Of your brother's visions."

THIRTEEN: *THE PEAR-SHAPED MAN*

MAGGIE WALKED slowly behind the unearthly duo, arms folded across her chest. She fought to keep the bile from rising in her stomach. Failed and spit a small sour stream. She wiped her mouth absently with the back of her hand.

Duma turned and looked at the ground. He gave her a sad smile like one gives when one sees a long lost friend at a funeral. She wished Harold was there to share with her like they'd shared everything for damn near fifty years. But he was gone, and so was her little brother.

Harold had always told her she was the strong one, his rock. But she knew in her heart that it was the other way around. And she needed him now. For this walk up the stairs to Victor's place, the place of her brother's death, grew unbearably heavier with each step. She stopped and fell to one knee. Tears welled in her eyes, despite her best efforts to stop them.

He will not see me cry, she thought. Ever again.

Or cower.

But somewhere inside her she knew that was only a half-truth, because the reality was that she was scared.

In that moment, on her knees she prayed to a God she had loved, cursed and even told a joke or two with in her lonely moments.

Maggie had been raised Catholic, but Harold had talked her out of that nonsense with a few well-placed anecdotes. As it turned out though, she had found the Baptists to also be lacking, especially in their sense of humor. And despite her best attempts, Maggie could never reconcile her faith with the science she often read about: The dinosaurs, evolution vs. creation, the "creation" book of Genesis. All these things seemed to hold her back from joining what she thought for the most part were a bunch of ignorant fools.

So they quit tithing and instead turned to surprising various nonprofit organizations with anonymous donations: Theater, art, cancer and most recently, heart research.

They did attend church, but on what they called their "after hours" schedule. They would arrive at any number of churches just as they were unlocked, or after services; they would find a place and pray together. They would also share things they had never told anyone. After 50 years, they still managed to come up with new stories. Sometimes they would sing. Harold had a beautiful voice, soft and on key. Generally.

It had been her favorite time of the week.

And she never felt so safe as when she was with Harold in those churches. Listening to his rendition of *Come Rain or Shine.*

She grabbed the rail and used it to hoist herself step by step. Duma offered her support and together they surmounted the final stairs. She expected to find yellow police tape X'ed across the door.

But it was clean.

Lucifer leaned against the door.

"He had boarded it up, Lucifer," Duma said.

But to his surprise, Lucifer opened it quite easily. They entered.

The smell of ammonia hit Maggie's nose. She sneezed. It was not what she expected. A clean blanket covered the bed. Boxes littered the room like forgotten mason stones, and the bookshelves housed little more than dust. A handful of wooden canvas frames leaned against the wall. Blank paintings, starving for an artist's blood. On the walls, paint-fingerprinted picture frames showcased ghost canvases matted with strips of sliced out paintings.

"It seems we are not the only ones interested in Victor's paintings," Lucifer said.

"He was quite talented," Duma said.

"Tortured," Lucifer said.

Someone was whistling.

"Hello?" Maggie said.

A pear-shaped man, cradling a box of books, turned, the corner from the hallway and stopped dead in his tracks. His face was long, with ears that stuck out too far; his hair was cropped short and some mark adorned his forehead. His paint-splattered overalls hung loose around his legs, but not his bottom or bulging stomach area as the grungy sleeveless T-shirt he wore underneath revealed body builder's arms.

"Oh, hey."

And then he dropped the box, which hit the floor with a resounding thud echoing off the barren walls. He turned abruptly and ran out the back door onto the balcony and jumped over the edge, arms windmilling.

Duma and Lucifer gave chase and leapt over the balcony railing also, without hesitation. Maggie rushed and leaned over the railing.

She expected to see the human pear with broken legs, surrounded by two angels not of mercy. But instead, the stranger was running.

Lucifer and Duma pursued.

The man moved faster than his shape would have suggested. He cut through the decrepit courtyard. Old lawn clippings and twigs kicked up in his wake. A swimming pool, green with stagnation, lay in his path. Maggie thought the man would go around the chain link fence, but instead he kicked open the gate. It swung hard, sending a small ripple effect down the length of the fence.

Duma was only a few yards behind, and closing. Lucifer was closing faster.

He's going to dive into the pool. "Don't hurt him," Maggie said.

The man crouched on the run and launched his body like a long jumper. Duma followed, arms coming down to hook the man's shoulders. The man's right foot hit the water and broke through the green and brown layer of muck; his left hit, but came back out as though the water was made of sponge.

Duma hit the water and disappeared in a splash beneath the surface. Lucifer jumped into the air and exploded into a flock of ravens flying across the water.

The man continued to pump his legs as though he was walking in a knee-deep snowdrift. He took a step onto solid ground on the other side, and continued to run.

The birds flew up, spiraling around their prey.

The man came to the rusty fence, but there wasn't another gate. He planted a foot into the links and began to climb. Maggie could see his muscles bulging even from the balcony. And then he slipped, hitting his head on the top cross pole.

"Ouch," he said, matter-of-factly. He quit climbing and touched his hand to his head. A tiny gash on his forehead wept blood.

The ravens spiraled around the man morphing back into a man's shape.

The pear-shaped man wiped his hand on his overalls and grinned. "You weren't too quick. I was quicker."

Lucifer brought his hand back.

Maggie closed her eyes.

Lucifer froze.

"That's right. You weren't expecting that, were you? I didn't think so. Nosiree." A small chuckle. "I think you better check on your friend. Don't look like he's having a good swim."

Maggie opened her eyes.

Duma was struggling to keep afloat, his broken wings hindering his progress.

"Don't figure he needs to breathe as much, but he looks pretty silly."

Astonishingly, Lucifer lowered his hand. Went and attended to the thrashing Duma.

The man jumped up and down and clapped his hands. "I guess I need to get my books." He started walking around the pool, back towards the apartment. He looked up. Waved to Maggie.

She waved back, puzzled.

∞

"And you would be?" Duma said, shaking his wings and body like a dog's. Water sprayed the room. Lucifer gave him a stern look.

Maggie found a kitchen towel and handed it to Duma.

The man sat on one box and flipped through another. His lips moved as he silently read the spines. He furrowed his brow on some, nodded his head in approval at others.

Duma cleared his throat.

"Oh, hey," the man said, and smiled. "Sorry."

"Who are you?" Maggie said.

"Could I have a bandage for my head?" He pointed to the small cut on his forehead. "It smarts."

Maggie reached into her purse and pulled out a small hiker's first aid bag. She gave him a small Band-Aid.

"Thank you," the man said, tearing it open and tucking the trash neatly into his pocket. "Bet you got a snake-bite kit in there as well." He glanced at Duma and Lucifer and then laughed softly again. "Bet you thought you could catch

me, huh? You wouldn't have, but I slipped." He turned to Maggie. "You used to torture Victor when he was small by pinning him down and dropping June bugs in his hair."

"I'm sorry, do I know you?" Maggie said, stepping forward.

"Nathan Pouge. Your brother called me Mr. Pouge."

"Did you go to my brother's church?"

He laughed again. Softly.

"Where are the paintings?"

He shrugged his shoulders. "Great, weren't they? Victor was great. People don't appreciate people with gifts like Victor's."

"You were taking the books," Maggie said. "I assume you were taking the paintings also."

"I'm supposed to take the books. That's what Victor told me to do. He was very specific about his instructions."

"And what exactly were those instructions?" Maggie asked.

"Victor knew something bad was coming. Something very bad. Bless Victor. I hadn't seen him in almost a couple of years. Not since he moved here. He would send me a Christmas card though, every year. A hand-painted original. *To my friend, Mr. Nathan Pouge.* That's me. Every year, but then he told me he was afraid he might have to go away, or something might happen to him. Sometimes he said things I didn't understand, like he was speaking in French or something. I asked some people; they didn't know what I was talking about. Just kind of looked at me funny. Like you're doing now, but that's okay. Boy, I was faster than you, wasn't I? But he said I had to do him a favor, I said I could, but a deal would be better if we barter for it. That way everyone's happy. So he said if he would call me when he needed the favor, that something was wrong and I needed to come here and clean up his place. I never thought he was talking about his body, but that's okay, cause we had a deal."

"And what did you get?" Duma said.

"His books. I got to get his books for the store. There's some okay stuff here— not really good stuff, but pretty okay. And pretty okay is better than just okay."

"Did you take his paintings?" Lucifer said. "We need them."

"No. Yes. Well, not all of them. When I got here I took a couple with me, not any in the frames. I don't know who took those— they weren't nice about it. No respect. See? They just ripped them right out of the frames, but I found a few in a box. A box of them rolled up. No frames or nothing."

"Where are those?" Lucifer said.

"What did you do with my brother's body?"

"Oh, don't worry Maggie, he got a proper burial. Very Christian."

"Could you show me where, Mr. Pouge?"

"Sure. It would be my honor."

"Mr. Pouge, I need to see those paintings," Lucifer said. "The life, excuse me, wellbeing of a friend of ours depends on it."

Mr. Pouge nodded thoughtfully. "I 'spect we could all pile into my truck and I could take you there."

"I want to see my brother's burial place."

"In due time, Maggie."

"Mr. Pouge," Maggie said. "How did you manage to run on water?"

"I'm special." He pointed to the silver circle on his forehead. "And if the devil don't like it, he can sit on a tack, sit on a tack." Mr. Pouge laughed to himself. And then stood. "Everyone grab a box. Hey, what did one shepherd say to the other shepherd?" Pause. "Let's get the flock out of here."

Duma laughed heartily and Maggie smiled.

They each grabbed a box and Lucifer stacked his on top of Duma's, who said nothing.

As they filed out of the apartment, Maggie nudged Duma. In a whisper, she asked: "Why is Lucifer so patient with Mr. Pouge?"

"Watch your words, Duma," Lucifer said.

"Do you forget why she is here, Prince of the World?" Duma said. "You chose her to do a job. She is supposed to be inquisitive."

"Somehow," Maggie said. "I don't believe Lucifer has learned Mercy so quickly."

"Oh no, Maggie, Mr. Pouge was not granted mercy," Duma said.

"It's that thing on his forehead," Maggie said.

"Yes."

"What is it?"

"The Mark of Cain."

FOURTEEN: *HOUSE OF POUGE*

TWELVE FLOOR-TO-CEILING oak bookshelves lined the walls of Nathan Pouge's small house.

Maggie whistled in admiration and ran a finger over the spines as she glanced at a number of them.

Mr. Pouge rushed up behind her, handkerchief out, wiping where Maggie had touched. "Please, the grease from your fingers."

"This is a breathtaking collection."

He laughed softly. "It's really all relative. This is nothing." He pulled out a bound periodical. "It's all relative. Says right here."

Maggie leaned over his shoulder as Mr. Pouge opened the book with it laying flat on his hand. He'd put out a handkerchief over it and turned the pages carefully at the corner. The book was an original copy of *The Special Theory of Relativity* by Einstein.

"He tossed out the part about gravitational waves," Mr. Pouge said. "But he was right there, too. Of course he'd rather play the violin than talk physics. You don't have to have music for physics, but you do have to have physics for music." He stared at Maggie, waiting for an acknowledgement.

She patted his shoulder and nodded.

He grinned and shook his head and put the book back, careful not to dent any of the corners.

"I've been collecting for awhile. A long while. Pick them up here and there. Estate sales, garage sales. Used book stores. They're from everywhere, all these books. Like discarded souls. Or people you pass in your life, but you really don't know what's on the inside unless you open them up. You can't judge a book by its cover. Pretty profound huh? Have you ever thought about that? Unless, of course, you're buying or selling, and then you do have to take into account the cover." He nodded to himself. "Yes, you do."

"Do you know what the Book of Life is?" Maggie said.

"Yes, I do."

"You don't happen to have it, do you?"

"Nope."

"Are you certain? There's a shitload lot of books."

"Yes and yes." He blew his nose with a tissue, so hard his ears wiggled. "Pick a bookcase, pick a shelf, pick a number." He closed his eyes.

"Sixth shelf, sixth row, Seventh book."

"A first edition of *A Prayer for Owen Meany*. One of my personal favorites."

"You are correct."

"Now you try," he said, indicating Lucifer.

"Let us see those paintings."

"You're no fun, *ha-satan*," Mr. Pouge said, and rolled to his feet.

∞

Mr. Pouge lugged in ten boxes of rolled canvases and placed them carefully in a semicircle in the middle of his living room. He dropped the last box and laughed to himself. Patted a huge bicep. "Yes, indeed."

They each took a box and began unrolling.

"Most of them are worthy of a frame, but I'm no carpenter. Nope." He sat cross-legged by Maggie. Touched his forehead where the gash was. Took off the Band-Aid. "How's it look?"

"You can hardly see it."

He nodded, rolling the small bandage into a ball between thick fingers and tucked it into his pocket. "So what are we looking for?"

"A friend," Maggie said.

"What's his name?"

"Andrew Honeybone," Duma said. "He's a lawyer, I think. A dead one."

"That's an interesting name," Mr. Pouge said. "So we're looking for a body."

"A walking one," Lucifer said.

"Oh, one of those." Mr. Pouge turned to Maggie. "So tell me about your friend."

"I reckon I really don't know much about him," Maggie said. "He said his wife was pregnant."

"What's his favorite ice cream?"

"I don't know."

"Another book unopened." Nathan Pouge shook his head. "So many of them."

Maggie unrolled another painting as Nathan Pouge droned on about various topics, always referencing them to a book whose exact location came to him with the certainty of a phone number.

Maggie nodded minimal encouragers to keep him talking. She liked the unique rhythm of his voice; it was not unlike Harold's when singing. She unrolled another painting and stopped short. She felt a tightening in her chest. She quickly rerolled the canvas and handed it to Pouge. "Please, destroy this one," she whispered.

Pouge stared at her blankly, but took it.

"Please."

She looked at the others. Duma cocked an eyebrow, but said nothing.

The phone rang. Pouge answered it. "Yes okay. Yes." He gently placed the receiver back as though he was laying an egg on a bed of nails. "Fellows, I have to go to work. They need me at the store."

"Are these *all* the paintings?" Lucifer said, the end of 'paintings' hissing long like a serpent's warning.

"I think there's enough for everyone," Mr. Pouge said. "Don't you think?"

Lucifer flew to his feet, hooked a book case with each hand and pulled down. They teetered for a second and then crashed to the floor like thunder, the books spilling into chaos.

"No," Pouge screeched. "You're hurting them." He picked up a few, gingerly touching corners here and there, shaking his head. He gently began to lay them out like casualties at a triage site. "How would you like your story to be treated like this, Mr. Morning Star?"

Duma and Maggie started to help.

"Be careful with them," Pouge said. "Very careful."

Lucifer crumpled in a corner, like an embarrassed child.

"You didn't have to do that," Pouge said.

"Oh no?" Lucifer said, and picked up a book and snapped its spine.

Pouge shrieked again. "Why are you doing this?"

"You may be carrying the Mark, but your precious children are not."

Then he flew into a rage, destroying book after book. Duma took Maggie by the shoulder and backed her into the relative safety of the small kitchen.

"Why," Pouge cried. "Why?"

"Damn you, Mika'il," Lucifer raged. "What have you done with our corpse?"

"Oh." Pouge perked up. "You're looking for a corpse? About yea high?"

"Have you seen him?"

"Got a gaping hole in his belly?"

"Yes," Duma said. "That's him. Where did you see him?"

Pouge and Maggie exchanged glances, and then Pouge carefully removed a rubble stack of torn pages and covers and spines from one of the boxes of paintings. "Eighth box, fifth roll, number two." He pulled out the rolled canvas and unfurled the painting.

Depicted in an impressionistic style was Honeybone, hanging upside down from a gray tree, against a light gray sky above a dark gray earth.

"That's him," Maggie said. "Why didn't you show us

this sooner?"

"You got a habit of asking the wrong questions."

Lucifer stared deeply at the painting, his face loosing into a passive, introspective mask.

Sidling up next to him Duma looked at the painting and then to Lucifer, who continued to gaze at the grayness.

The air crackled with a foreign electricity. Maggie could not quite place the vibe.

"Where's that?" Pouge asked, genuinely curious.

"Paradise," Duma said.

"Awfully gray."

The two stood silently as the remains of dozens of damaged books pooled around their ankles like a shallow puddle.

Maggie bent down as best she could. Pouge nodded and pulled back his coveralls just enough to show her where he'd hidden the painting she'd asked him to dispose.

"I'm sorry," Maggie said, handing him a book with the creased title, *The Madness of Crowds.*

"They're only books," Mr. Pouge said, neutrally.

"Shall we depart," Lucifer said, gritting his teeth and gesturing to the door in a sweeping motion.

Duma scratched his soft chin, staring at the gray painting. "I do not wish to visit there, Lucifer."

"Little One," Lucifer chided.

"I have to go to work," Pouge said. "I'll escort you

out."

A small sound escaped from the back of Duma's throat.

"Wait," Maggie said. "Mr. Pouge, I know we asked you if you have the book, but *did* you have the book?"

"The Book of Life?" Pouge said. "Yessiree."

Lucifer stepped forward as far as Pouge's round gut would allow. "Where did you get it from?"

"Victor had it among his collection. It was right under your nose," Pouge said. "With the other books."

Lucifer let out a bloodcurdling scream. The light bulb overhead shattered.

Pouge touched his forehead tracing the silver circle.

"Where is the book now?"

"At the bookstore. That's where I work," Pouge said, picking up the shattered pieces of the light bulb from the fallen books. "At the best bookstore in the world, the Wellspring."

"Why did we have to sit here and wade through these?" Lucifer said, tearing through a handful of half-finished canvases.

"You didn't ask the right questions? Haven't all day," Pouge said. "Maggie, she's the smart one."

"Mr. Pouge, could you take us to the Wellspring?"

"I suppose," he said, adjusting his bulging overalls. "What about your friend, Honeybone?"

Duma looked at Lucifer.

"We do not need him now."

Duma nodded in agreement, but his eyes lingered on the painting. He ran his fingers over it slowly, feeling the texture of the mountains and valleys of a bleak, tortured terrain.

"We can't leave him there," Maggie said.

Lucifer glowered at her. "Mr. Pouge, if you will."

"There is a season," Mr. Pouge said. "Turn, turn, turn."

FIFTEEN: *THE WELLSPRING*

THE ODOR OF PULP smelled to Maggie like ripe fruit.

Memories of a family trip to a cabin by a lake filled her head. The images were vivid in color and detail; the bumblebee by the flowers on the stair, the bent nail on the railing, rust on its top side. She saw her dad, his stomach still flat, in tight swimming trunks; her mother hanging the beach towels on a line strung between two oaks. And the hot narrow cement walkway beneath her feet.

She had not thought of that place in years. A musty smell filled her nose; the "dead spider smell," as she had called it. The nostalgia surprised her, and then it suddenly faded. The colors became drab and fuzzy around the edges. She sneezed, and the image was lost to her.

"Bless you," the owner said. He stepped around from his wooden counter. He was a short dark man with a clean-shaven head and light growth of beard. His eyes were a light caramel color, sharp behind small-framed glasses. He wore a gray work shirt, similar to one she'd bought Harold a few years ago, and blue jeans. "Dusting is another item I need to add to my list."

"Dusting." Mr. Pouge whipped out a small pad from his overalls and jotted something down. "I'll do it."

"Have you owned this place long?" Maggie said.

The owner smiled. "Yes." He held his hand out, first to Maggie. She took it. It was warm, dry and very gentle. She gripped hard, and he responded likewise. A tingle ran up her arm. He released first, but the tingle remained as though she had been lightly tapped on the elbow.

He did not hold his hand out to Lucifer, who stood just inside the doorway under a string of shiny bells.

Maggie struggled to find her voice. "Quite a collection."

"I sell mostly to collectors. People fascinated with history or the novelty of owning a book that someone read two hundred years ago."

"I got paperbacks made three months ago that are falling apart."

"Book binding used to be a true craft, Maggie."

Lucifer walked to the back of the store, running his

fingers along the spines. "Impressive, Yeshundra."

"Is there something in particular I can help you find, an old Shakespeare book of sonnets?" He smiled wryly. "Milton, perhaps?"

"I'm seeking a special book," Lucifer said. "One of a kind."

"Could you give me a description of it?"

"There as many descriptions for this book as there are stars," Lucifer said. "But I will know it, by touch."

"By touch."

"Shhh," Lucifer said. Eyes closed, he turned gracefully around the corners. Occasionally, he stopped and let a finger linger on a book as though checking for a pulse.

Trailing behind Lucifer, Maggie sneezed and coughed up more of the brown stuff. "Place could use a cleanin'."

"Some of this dust is older than you," Pouge said.

"Great. I'll bake a cake."

∞

A shaft of light from the store front window illuminated a cloud of dust particles, whirling this way and that. Maggie stuck her hand out into the sun, like a cat, and felt a momentary throbbing between her legs.

"Daylight. Afternoon."

"Pardon," Lucifer said, not breaking his pace.

"My parents owned a cabin by a lake in Oklahoma. We used to go there every Fourth of July with friends of the family. I used to sun myself on the screened-in porch. There were two beds, high off the ground, and under each of them a pull out bed. My boyfriend, Ted something, and I lost our virginity on one of those musty beds while everyone else went for a walk. I sneezed as he climaxed. Both of us had a good laugh at that."

"Hmm."

"But we lay afterwards with the sun warming the bed, grinning at our small triumph. So sneaky. I was a little sore, but I remember the sun being so warm. I took a moment to look at all my surroundings to absorb all the little details, to cherish them. But the last several years, I couldn't have told you if it was in the daylight or at night."

"I found something," Duma said.

Lucifer turned.

Duma cradled two books. Both were leather, with faded pages. "For Honeybone. I believe he said he was a lawyer." He handed Maggie a thick tome.

The Law of Heaven.

"That's very thoughtful," Maggie said.

"It is not the Book, but listen to this:" He cleared his throat and read from the other book. "'Say heavenly power where shall we find such love. Which of ye be mortal to redeem man's mortal crime and just the unjust to save dwells in all heaven charitie so dear—'"

"'He ask'd but all the Heavenly Quire stood mute,'" the owner, Yeshundra said. "'And Silence was in heaven on man's behalf.'"

"Ah, Milton..." A man had entered from a back room. A bundle of books hung under his arm. He set the load down gently on the counter, nodded to Yeshundra, and loosened his priest collar. "Thank you." He pulled out a pair of sunglasses from his shirt pocket and put them on. Nodded to Maggie. "Ma'am."

The front door jingled as he left. Before the dissonant notes died, another man in black entered and walked to the backroom. His graying hair was pulled back into a loose ponytail and his salt and pepper beard was matted with knots. The only jewelry he wore was a leather thong around his neck, attached to a worn leather pouch. With a small wave to the owner, he entered and closed the door behind him.

"What's behind there?" Lucifer said, eyeballing the back door.

"A reading room."

Lucifer turned. "A reading room for?"

"Books. The *old* ones."

"Older than these?" Maggie said. "Can we take a gander?"

"I'm sorry. Preferred customers. But I can assure you

the book you are looking for is not in there."

"How about a quick look see," Maggie said.

"Perhaps some other time."

"I think not." Lucifer stepped forward, Yeshundra moved to block his way. Lucifer towered over him by a good two feet. "I could make you move, little man, if I so desired."

"I have been gracious and accommodating," Yeshundra said. His eyes seemed to turn dark and his voice dropped an octave. "To you and your companions. And now you assume this posture?" He clucked his tongue.

Maggie wheeled back. The sun disappeared and a shadow fell over her arm. Gooseflesh followed.

Lucifer smirked.

A second passed.

An eternity.

"You have a short beard. Surprisingly, matching your popular depictions."

"The Byzantine artists added the beard," Yeshundra said, not backing down. "Does it suit me, Light Giver?"

"Allow me passage to this back room."

"I will grant it. Not out of fear, but respect." He stepped aside. "Do you understand that?"

Lucifer bowed slightly.

The door opened with a whisper.

Inside, antique bookshelves reached twenty feet high;

long tables dominated the center of the room with high-backed chairs from different periods of time. A small group of men occupied a number of chairs. Small stacks of books, both open and closed, lined the center of the table. As far as Maggie could make out, the group consisted of an eclectic mix of Hasidic men, a few oriental, and some blacks. Many took notes, their brows furrowed in concentration. The street noise disappeared. Maggie felt the same warmth from the previous room although this one was windowless.

Lucifer entered the room. All looked up at him. A few stared; others hastily exited. Within a dozen heartbeats only one man remained, the man with the ponytail and beard who had just arrived. Lucifer ignored him, his attention on the vast number of books and scrolls.

Maggie came further into the room with the rest of the group. The musty smell was stronger and more pungent. She looked at the row of books on a shelf at her eye level. Some of the spines were inscribed with silver, some with gold, others had faded to an unrecognizable hue. She reached out and touched a book older than she could have imagined. None of the spines were in English.

"Hebrew. Aramaic. Greek. Some Latin," Ponytail said, his eyes flicking back and forth between Maggie and Lucifer. "The later translations."

"What are these?"

"The greatest stories ever told."

"Bibles?"

"That would be a misnomer. Although I can see why you would assume that. These are the original Gospels."

"First editions, huh?" Maggie said with awe. "Damn, that's pretty old."

Yeshundra laughed.

"A lot of the original Jewish texts, and a hodgepodge of others." Ponytail ticked them off on his fingers. "The Akhmim Codex, *Heptamerson, seu Elemntia, The Book of Adam, Raziel ha-Malach, Codex Apocryphus Novi Testamenti.*" His eyes settled on Lucifer. "But I doubt any of those would interest you."

"I seek the Book of Life," Lucifer said.

"I must admit I did not expect you to be so concerned with these matters." Yeshundra scratched his beard. "Most interesting." He chuckled.

"Would you care to share with us," Lucifer said, as his eyes scanned the shelves. "Son of Mary."

"I played you. On stage. I've been getting involved with some of the community theatre. We did a Passion Play. I was you. I think you would have been impressed," he said. "The local critic called my character flat and boring."

"Then you know what it is like to walk in my shoes."

"Perhaps."

"The Book, Yeshundra..."

"What, oh, yes. The Book of Life," Yeshundra said. "In its last incarnation it was lightly tanned. Crisp papyrus pages. The spine and cover bound with the hair of the firstborns. Reinforced with Silver from the core of the City."

"Give it to me," Lucifer said.

"I can't do that."

"Give me the book, and I will allow you to continue your new life unhindered. Theater and this bookstore."

"The Presence has invested some trust in you, eh?" He tapped his finger against his lip in thought. "Or is it something other than that? What did they promise you, Morning Star? Without the Book, the Revelation cannot happen. There would be an Alpha without an Omega— is that not something the old Morning Star would wish? Perhaps you seek the book to destroy it."

"There are others seeking the book," Duma said. "Others have fallen without Blessing. Mika'il leads them."

Yeshundra chewed on this. "Perhaps he does not trust the Morning Star."

"Perhaps Mika'il plans to lead his own revolution," Lucifer said. "The first Fall was his idea, after all."

Duma said nothing.

"You dance more in the grayness now, Light Giver," Yeshundra said. "But if you do seek the Book to return it to

Heaven, I wonder, what are you receiving in exchange?" He thought in silence for a moment. "Yes, that would have to be it, wouldn't it?"

More silence.

Lucifer stepped closer. Ponytail stood, but Yeshundra backed him off with a small gesture.

"Yeshundra. Give me the book."

"Oh yes, now I see."

"Do you see I am prepared to destroy you?"

"Destroy me? Father would be quite mad. But go ahead if you must. It has never stopped you before."

Lucifer rounded on the table and splintered its oak top with a fist.

He's just a spoiled child, Maggie thought.

The books and scrolls collapsed in on themselves with the gravity of a dying star. "Give me the goddamn book."

"Is that supposed to be funny?"

"Mayhap, I shan't kill you but reenact the last temptation," Lucifer said.

"Boring, and not enjoyable for your guests, I'm sure," Yeshundra said.

There was an odor about Lucifer now, Maggie thought. She recognized it as desperation. "Give me the book."

"Yes, the Book."

"The Book of Life."

Yeshundra sat casually in a throne-like chair and glanced at the pile of books. "I sold it."

SIXTEEN: *THE DEAL*

"I DON'T UNDERSTAND," Maggie said. "Why would you sell it? Why would you even have it? Did you steal it?"

A hush fell over the room. Ponytail stopped picking up the scattered books.

"No, I did not steal the book."

"Did one of the Sopheriel twins give it to you?" Duma asked. "Have they truly fallen?"

"That question will be answered when you see them," Yeshundra said. He took off his glasses and cleaned them with the tail of his shirt. "Mr. Pouge, would you be so kind as to replace a box or two of returns?"

"Of course I would be so kind," Pouge said, and busied himself with requested tasks.

"Excellent help," Yeshundra replied. "Sharp as a tack."

"The Book," Maggie said. "How did you get it?"

"I understand the nature of jealousy, of pride—temptation, if you will. It is a powerful thing. It has conquered nations, divided them, split Heaven itself; a key example standing here in our modest bookstore." He pretended to look over their shoulders. "I thought there was another with you. Andrew Honeybone, I believe."

"He is no longer with us," Lucifer said.

"Cryptic. I shouldn't have expected anything but." He placed his glasses carefully back on and quite tactfully said, "Where is he?"

Duma turned and left the room.

Yeshundra cocked an eyebrow and followed him out. The rest of the group, save Ponytail, did the same.

The little angel approached the counter head down. Held out the rolled painting.

With great care, Yeshundra took it and unrolled it on the counter top, unmindful of the books stacked there.

Mr. Pouge cleared his throat and moved the books with a smile.

Yeshundra adjusted his glasses and blinked his eyes several times. "And the Lord God said, 'The man has now become like one of us, knowing good and evil. He must not be allowed to reach out his hand and take also from the tree of life and eat and live forever. So the Lord God banished him from the Garden to work the ground from which he had been taken. After he drove the man out, he placed on the east side of the garden cherubim and a flaming sword flashing back and forth to guard the way to the tree of life.'" He paused, and said solemnly. "I'm paraphrasing, of course."

Garden, Maggie thought to herself. "The Garden of Eden? Honeybone is there?"

"Hanging from the tree of life it would appear."

"To whom did you sell the book?" Lucifer said.

"A spectacular woman. Quite remarkable. Although I did not catch her name."

Maggie thought of the cop novels her husband used to read. "Do you have a check, or a receipt for a credit card?"

Mr. Pouge stepped out from behind a rack of books. "Cash only, please," he said, pointing to a sign that stated quite simply: CASH ONLY PLEASE.

"I tell you what, Serpent," Yeshundra said, slyly. "Bring me Honeybone."

"And you will give us the Book?"

"I cannot give you what I do not have." "You'll give us—"

"Perhaps— bring me Honeybone and we'll see. What choice do you have?"

"I'd like to stay here," Duma said, softly. "If you don't mind."

"Ah Duma, the silent one. 'Jophiel' wasn't it, before the Fall?"

"Yes, milord."

"'Jophiel,'" Maggie said. "I don't understand."

"This Little One was once not so little," Yeshundra said. "He knew your parents, Maggie McCreedy."

"Frank and—"

"Not those parents, Maggie," Duma said. "I escorted Adam and Eve out of the Garden. Not to mention Lilith before them. But she left of her own accord."

"Quite a spirit," Yeshundra said. "Not unlike yours, Maggie."

Maggie stood, a bit gobsmacked.

"So I bring back Honeybone—"

"He is your responsibility."

"And?"

"We'll have supper. Chat."

Mr. Pouge stepped up behind Yeshundra and whispered something in his ear. "Yes. Great idea."

Pouge handed him a small stack of books. "Maggie, it seems we have a few first editions of your early works. Would you be so kind as to sign them?"

The absurdity of the request brought her mind back. She found herself slipping into a more familiar exercise. "Of course, I'd be delighted." She took the first book, and turned to the dedication page.

For Harry.

She smiled. She took a pen from the counter and as the tip of the pen touched paper Yeshundra spoke matter-of-factly, "Trust not in the folly of angels."

Their eyes lingered for a moment. Pouge came up behind her, took her elbow and guided her away from the counter.

∞

For the next few minutes Lucifer leaned on the counter towards Yeshundra, who leaned neither towards or away; they engaged in a rather animated conversation.

Maggie regained her composure and became curious enough to find out the nature and magnitude of that conversation. She wandered toward them feigning interest in the books; both stopped talking and looked at her.

"Romance starts on the fifth shelf," Mr. Pouge said, guiding Maggie by the elbow again.

She resisted slightly. "I've had enough of that crap to last me forever."

"Really," Pouge said, disappointment in his voice. "Some of it is quite inventive. Quite life-affirming. It's no substitute for the Good Book though, nothing is. But that's a bit of a read; one can get 'lost' if one doesn't know how to read it."

Maggie nodded, and positioned herself so that she could continue to watch the duo.

"Do you think it's really Him?"

"Which one?"

"Yeshundra?"

"Oh yes."

"And the other, what do you think?"

"I don't know. Of course, how could I not," Maggie said. "He's right there, and what I saw him do to Honeybone…"

"Too bad you don't have his knife," Mr. Pouge said.

This statement caught Maggie by surprise. She said nothing, letting the words hang in the air.

"You could stab him through the heart with his own knife if you were quick enough, eh? I could. I'm quicker than him. Quick, quick," Mr. Pouge said. "For Victor."

Maggie put a hand on his arm, opened her mouth in protest, but found herself hesitating, nodding slightly.

"These are my thoughts, although I shouldn't be having them. I have to turn the other way." He scratched his long chin. "I destroyed the painting like you asked."

She envisioned Victor's last moments on earth. She looked back over to the odd couple and stared at the barely visible hilt of Lucifer's dagger.

Mr. Pouge laughed softly, shaking his head. He

repeated his statement about the painting.

"Thank you," she said, absently. She found herself taking a small step forward, eyes glued to the hilt.

The bell dangling over the front door sang as Duma opened it, pulling on his coat. "I'm going for a walk. The bells continued their hum, breaking Maggie from her trance. She shook her head and felt a little groggy.

"Have you heard the saying that Christianity would be great," Mr. Pouge said. "If it weren't for all the Christians?"

Maggie stifled a laugh and then went into a coughing spasm. Pouge tapped her lightly on the shoulder. She spit into her rag and pocketed it without looking.

"They are both magnificent, aren't they?" he said. "Like Greek sculptures."

"Except Yeshundra—"

"The Son of Man is dark. Not quite the discount outlet store Aryan version they sell down South, now is it?"

"It doesn't bother me—"

He hushed her with a finger to her lips. The scent of earth caught her nose. "I can watch him for hours," Pouge said, flexing a knotted arm. "Of course I have to. Sometimes he forgets they are books. He's quite gentle with the scrolls and bits of scrolls left in the back, but sometimes, he just forgets or doesn't care. So Maggie, what of your faith now?"

"Excuse me?"

"What is your devil's deal with the devil?"

"I thought I could write something that would make a difference."

"Despite your brother's death?"

"Something that would have an impact, something important."

He picked up a book. One of hers. "About 90,000, yes?" He paused. "Have you ever grasped that number? Imagine a sporting event. At an arena, filled with people. Scatter those people, they all have one thing in common. Your book. And they'll buy the next one. Because they care about what you have to say. Maybe to some of them it's a trivial distraction at the end of a long day, which makes it important."

"You lost me there."

"Yes, indeed." He read a passage out of her book and closed it. "Because of this paragraph, seventy-six women opted not to get a divorce, but to seek counseling. Three women left their abusive husbands. One of them died— but she died free. Without fear. One man began to write his wife poetry after having picked up one of your books his wife had left laying in the family car. They had been at a crossroads in their marriage." He shrugged. "I would hate to think of how many women are waiting to make a life decision based on Sapphire's answer to Lord Sterling. Yes, indeed."

"If they are waiting on that then they're idiots."

"Not all of them," Pouge said, sliding her book carefully back into its home slot on the shelf. "Have known a love as enduring and supportive as yours."

"Victor never found anyone."

"Then you were truly blessed," Pouge said. "But know this, as horrible and perhaps as unnecessary as his death was, his body was tranquil and without a sign of pained expression. He was truly at peace, and tonight he sleeps in the arms of the Lord."

Maggie sat down abruptly on a stepladder in the corner of the store and cried with a mix of pain and joy.

As if reading her emotions, "His was a just and good life, Maggie. You were a large part of that despite the silences that passed between you. Yes, indeed. There are always silences." He paused as if to reiterate his point. "I will show you his final resting spot. When all of this... questing is done. Yes, indeed."

Maggie dabbed her eyes, looked up to Mr. Pouge and said quietly, "Thank you." And then, "What about Harry? Where does he sleep?"

To which he just chuckled softly and smiled.

Maggie folded up her hanky and stuffed it back into her pocket.

"So, it's not really a matter of faith for you anymore.

You've met Him and *him*." He tapped his chin thoughtfully. "That makes it a little outside of itself. Almost—"

The front door bell sang again violently. Duma entered. "I'll go, but if we don't leave now, I may change my mind, so let's get the hell of out here."

SEVENTEEN: *EDEN*

A FIST SEIZED Maggie's entrails and squeezed them to jelly. The wind left her body, and she fought to take in the most shallow of breaths. Felt a lump of the brown stuff nesting at the back of her throat. Her ears rang, and her head pounded slowly with the tempo of her excited heart.

Her hip protested to no avail as a dark mass rose to meet her face— and then stopped.

Am I hovering? she thought.

She felt herself lowered slowly to the gray mass, which somewhere in the haze of her mind she realized must be the earth. She was laid gently on the ground; a force eased her into a sitting position, her head level with her knees. She vomited, clearing her airway. A soothing hand rubbed her back in a circular motion.

Her stomach rolled into itself, forcing the remaining contents onto the ground.

"Can't breathe," she gasped.

"You will be fine, Maggie," Duma said, somewhat distracted.

"God, let me die," she pleaded, using the one breath she was able to draw.

And then something warm came over her. A hand grasped hers. A tingle went up her arm, joined by a faint throbbing between her legs. She felt lightheaded, almost drunk. Chills washed over her and her wrinkled flesh became speckled with gooseflesh.

"Oh, Harold, you devil, I love you, too."

And in a voice so comfortable and familiar and crystal clear:

"Lassy, will you be my wife?"

And every pain Margaret McCreedy had ever known simply disappeared. She closed her eyes and reveled in pure joy.

She spun, holding her skirt, as the man lead her into a slow Waltz. But the timing was just a little off, and she stepped on his toe and giggled. She opened her eyes and smiled to apologize.

But there was no ballroom, no dance, no Harold.

Lucifer stood there, one hand holding hers, the other thrust into his coat pocket. "Feeling better?"

Maggie looked around confused and not a little embarrassed. "You did that?"

"We were losing you," Duma said. "How do you feel?"

"Like a fool," she said, but inhaled, absorbing the lingering smell of her old dance partner.

"You were quite graceful, if I might say."

Maggie spit and started to walk off. But Duma put a hand on her shoulder. "It would be best if you stuck with us."

Black sand parted casually under her feet, and the sky was not gray but bright, wasting its illumination on a bleak environment without texture or form. There was only a godlessness that expanded to the horizon.

"Barren," Maggie commented as flies began to buzz annoyingly around her head. She thought momentarily about turning down her hearing aid to alleviate some of the irritation. Duma held out a crooked arm for support as though an escort at a grand ball; Maggie took it for support, finding the sand quickly becoming tiresome for her legs and hip.

They walked for what seemed like hours but may have been only a fraction of that.

Suddenly Duma whispered: *"There."*

On the horizon was the painting she'd seen at the Wellspring, but it was as if a set of invisible hands were holding it up like a grand theatrical backdrop. A black tree dominated the scene. Something like an obscene fruit hung from it.

A cacophony reached their ears; hundreds of birds flew far overhead. They were absent of color, like coal; Maggie thought of fighter planes. Their formation creating symmetrical shapes in the sky morphing effortlessly, if not quietly. They continued to the horizon, shifting and expanding and contracting their patterns like a monochromatic kaleidoscope. And then they fell, pouring from the sky like black oil onto the solitary tree.

Lucifer and Duma exchanged a few words in a language not of this earth.

Maggie cocked a questioning eyebrow at the tree.

"Raphael, Metatron, or Sabbithiel."

"I've never heard of the last one."

"Yes, you have. By another name, not his mystery name," Duma said. "Michael."

Maggie's bowels loosened and she fought for control. "And if we don't get Honeybone back. We just scram, right? That's it, right?"

"Margaret McCreedy, if we do not get Honeybone back to the Wellspring we will not be able to find out the whereabouts of the Book from Yeshundra. If that happens, this world will see its streets run with rivers of blood, its children eaten and devoured by their mothers, and a plague of night and winter. The only warmth to be found will be in the belly of the freshly slain. For I am Prince of this World and have been told by the Presence to destroy those that would hinder my quest for the Book of Life. For without that book there will be no Judgment as foretold in the Revelation."

And then the cacophony about the tree reached such a crescendo that Maggie had to cover her ears. She could not hear her own screams, save for the burning in her throat.

And the first shape formed of the leaves of the tree of life and greeted the travelers. Waving a flaming sword, the shape spoke to Duma and said, "I am Cassiel, my brother, do you remember?"

"Yes, my brother, it was you and I who danced, you losing your sight and I flight."

"And here you are in the company of the Dragon, the serpent whose bitter wormwood would spoil the finest wine."

And he reared his head back and the roar was that of a lion. He raced to the west waving his flaming sword, his

sandaled feet touching not the earth.
And Duma answered with a roar
that unsettled the leaves of the Tree of Life.
He raced westward, following the smoking
trail of Cassiel's sword.

Michael stepped forward, eyes blazing. Lucifer tossed off his cloak, which billowed to the ground like an abandoned parachute. The two met like gladiators in an invisible coliseum. Maggie could hear their voices thunder and echo across the landscape as they spoke. The clouds darkened into a dense canopy, and in the distance, a pack of hyenas mocked them with laughter.

"My hate for you, Morning Star, is the strongest in Creation and rivals the Love I have for my Lord."

"In this painting, perhaps," Lucifer said. "Can you see I have not raised my hand against you? Can you see now and understand my nature? Or are you still so blind? Cassiel can see, and he has only one eye."

"It is a shame, brother," Michael said. "That you cannot see what I see."

"I see the chief celestial prince, who fell to earth without Blessing," Lucifer said. "I see a rebel angel."

"Nothing happens that is not His will."

Lucifer drew his dagger. "So be it."

And with that simple declaration, the celestial titans

moved forward for their confrontation born before man and his knowledge of jealousy, contempt, hate, good and evil.

It left Maggie with little justification for her own emotions, and a surreal feeling of detachment flooded her. She felt as though she were viewing the scene from slightly above the level of the earth.

Like a pair of condemned men, Michael and Lucifer continued their solemn walk towards one another and Maggie felt the strength and will to witness it leave her; she had also forgotten about Duma chasing his fate over the black sand. And although she was insignificant to the entities, Maggie realized a budding sense of belonging here. She was drawn to this place, a place she had neither seen nor felt in her dreams, but recognized only from a painting by a man she thought she knew.

Her brother.

She bent with a great effort and touched the sand. It was cool to the touch, and it seemed important to her to remember that fact. To remember the minutia of *that*. Despite the vast differences between herself and the denizens both human and reptilian, she felt she had truly come home. She wondered if it was but a tiny fraction of what Adam and Eve felt.

She didn't know if this euphoria and empathy for people long since returned to dust was related to the release of her fears. Fears which had haunted her for the last couple of years: Fear of death, fear of being alone, fear of not making a mark on this earth, of not leaving anything to be remembered by.

My life reduced to so many column inches in the back of an unread newspaper, she thought. To be reported missing here, generating a short string of articles read only by a few desperate for Sapphire. Perhaps she would live on without me, Maggie thought. The publishers could find many eager young writers to take up the thankless task.

Surprisingly, the thought of it turned her mouth bitter.

Let it go, Shorty.

Her head swam in euphoria as it came back to Harold. It always came back to Harold. Sweet, strong, funny Harry. Pouge had dodged her question about Harold's afterlife fate. Once it had only been a nagging concern that rarely bubbled past the level of conscious thought, forming only in the twilight of waking dreams. But now her faith became not a matter of choice, of belief, but simply a matter of whether to embrace or not to embrace.

I still have so many stupid questions...

The rival archangels collided and Eden shook, jarring Maggie back to her body. She turned her back on them, fleeing beyond the next rise in the land. Hyenas cackled, the crocs roared against instinct, and the sky flashed with ball lightning and deafening thunder.

She turned and looked back as had Lot's wife. A lightning strike flashed, turning her world to negative as ghost images danced on her weak retinas. She stumbled blindly, her hands out front for balance. Something caught her foot, and the heavens roared again. She fell to the ground and put her hands and arms over her head as if she were a little girl. The distant explosions continued, and between them she could make out another sound.

The scream of angels.

The scream was unlike anything she had ever heard before. She slowly lifted her head and dared look.

Cassiel and Duma?

She strained her poor eyes, but the erratic strobing light and sudden shadows made it extremely hard. Finally, some movement down near the bottom of the rise caught her attention. It was the two angels, their heads thrown back and screaming.

My God.

Their bodies writhed and convulsed violently.

They're killing each other.

Another sustained flash exposed them and she realized they were not fighting, but had locked wings and were rutting like animals. Their actions found the rhythm of the thunder and lighting, pounding into each other like a tribal ritual; their screams joined the cacophony, becoming part of a great celestial machine. She sat back and watched them with fascination. As the thunder boomed louder and echoed longer, they became more tender, more graceful, more... artful. For a split second Duma's swooning face was illuminated in stark contrast. She thought he was looking her way. She held her breath, the flash died, and his look of ecstasy disappeared once again into the shadows.

She did not chance another look over her shoulder; this battle existed beyond simple facts, thoughts, or perceptions available to her. A thousand recorded versions could evolve of this final stand; myths, legends, and apocryphal tales, stretching from the Ninth Level to the Seventh Circle-- and who could say that any or all of them were wrong.

Later, sitting on her porch back home, Maggie McCreedy would find that this simple sentence satisfied her as a storyteller:

And Lucifer and Michael wrestled
on the black sands
of a once green Eden.

A final crashing sound raced from the Tree of Life like a shockwave, stunning animals, humans and insects. Patches of sand turned to black glass, which in turn shattered, peppering the terrain with millions of jagged razors. When the screaming inside Maggie's head died down she turned to the east. Saw only the back of Morning Star; his wings, spread to their full glorious width, blocked out most of the branches and Honeybone. She picked herself up.

Where is Michael?

She couldn't see anything. Overhead the clouds folded in on themselves, imploding into ghost wisps and revealing a starry twilight. As though stepping out of a storm shelter, she crested the hill with slow, painful steps.

She struggled to come up behind Lucifer. Her curiosity, once just a mischievous trait, now returned, consumed her. Maggie stumbled, cutting her hands on the splintered sand. Tiny shards shredded the knees of her jeans. The blood ran from her hands freely, though she hardly noticed. A dog-like creature howled in the darkness. Once again she picked herself up, her lungs burning.

Finally, she reached Lucifer; his wings still spread like great onyx sails. Honeybone hung to her right, upside down. Below him was a small pile of flesh that the last shockwave had sloughed off. He was screaming.

"WHY? WHY? HE WAS GOING TO RELEASE ME? WHY? WHY?"

The tone and terror of his screams tore her out of her trance. Her palms flared with pain. She rolled up her shirttails to stifle the blood.

Lucifer's wings lowered slowly. He looked over his shoulder at her. "Did you note that, scribe?" he said in a voice that loosened her bowels.

A hyena laughed.

Lucifer's right hand was around Michael's throat. Michael's eyes stared into Lucifer's. Maggie couldn't see Morning Star's left hand. Then, as his wings lowered still, it was unveiled; it grasped his dagger tightly, the hilt to the rear of Lucifer's fist and the blade disappearing into Michael's heart.

The final thunder had been Michael's last words.

Lucifer eased the pressure of his arm on Michael's neck and withdrew the blade.

Honeybone sobbed. *"Itsadream itsadream itsadreamitsa..."*

Michael's body slid almost gracefully down the tree, stripping it of the remaining bark that his body had sheltered.

Lucifer stood there in silence, the ambient sounds of the Lake denizens starting to come back to life like a subdued musical score.

A hyena with xylophone ribs emerged from the darkness of the lakeshore, his teeth blazing. A deep guttural rumble emerged from somewhere in its bowels; a rope of saliva touched the ground.

Maggie gasped, and took a step back. Lucifer's arms

dropped. He advanced.

The stray's snout swung from side to side, looking first at the Fallen it wished to claim.

Lucifer stepped forward again, his lips curling around his teeth.

Maggie crossed herself.

The hyena leapt, snout pointed towards Lucifer's neck. Lucifer's arm suddenly appeared, catching the dog by its throat. With a movement so swift Maggie was not entirely sure she had actually seen it. Lucifer drove the hyena's body to the ground.

Ribs cracked, and the dog's tongue hung at an awkward angle with its wounded yelp. Lucifer kept his hand on the panting hyena's throat kneeling down with the effort.

The hyena's ribs seemed to pulse as its breath became harsh and ragged. Its eyes rolled wildly in their sockets, its breath visible.

Lucifer's hand tightened as he bent closer to the pointed head. The panting grew quicker, but shallow; the ribs danced less, its bowels evacuated, and the smell of feces filled the air.

Maggie noticed that Lucifer's breathing pattern took the rhythm of the animal's. And then his chest ceased its movement also.

His free hand went to the dog's ribs, touched each one

of them and stroked the fur laying it smooth. Then Lucifer's head lowered to the hyena's mouth, and with a finger wiped away the blood and saliva. Gently, he picked something from its ear. Continued to stroke its fur and then whispered something in a language Maggie couldn't comprehend.

Suddenly, the hyena coughed. Something wet and globular splattered from its mouth. Lucifer cradled its head, held it for a moment, and then let go. The dog gagged and barked a wet grumble, which became clearer with the next bark. It rolled to its feet, wobbly on newborn legs.

Lucifer traced a sign on its fur.

The dog licked Lucifer's open hand. Then, with a last look, it trotted back into the darkness toward Lake Turkana.

Lucifer stayed, squatting on his haunches.

Duma rejoined the group alone. He and Maggie exchanged looks but said nothing as they watched the hyena disappear back into the darkness. Duma stared at the body of Michael for a moment.

Maggie couldn't read his passive face. He began to cut down a whimpering Honeybone.

"He was going to release me."

Lucifer's hand went to his head and pushed against his temple as though fighting off an excruciating headache. Something wet slid down his cheek, just catching the starlight.

Maggie struggled for a moment to find her voice. Softly: "How do you feel?"

Lucifer continued to stare at the body slumped against the cold sand. "As when Cain slew Abel."

Maggie shifted her weight, withdrew a half-smoked cigar from her jacket. She lit up and sucked in a lung full and exhaled slowly. "Now what?"

Lucifer stood and went to the body of Michael, and with some effort draped it over his shoulder with a surprising gentleness. "I bury my brother."

Maggie chewed on the end of her cigar for a moment. Nodded. "I know a place."

Duma drew a circle around the group in the sand as some of the tribal denizens of Turkana crested a hill in the distance, silhouetted against the starlight.

A melodic chant floated over the sand, and Duma responded to the call with a few soft words of his own, his head bowed.

The voices became distant as Maggie's stomach turned itself inside out in protest again.

EIGHTEEN: *THE RANCH*

ERRANT SPARKS escaped from the fireplace flitting here and there as Maggie stoked it. Lucifer slumped in the corner, his fingers steepled beneath his nose. He had been sitting there for hours. The only thing he'd said was in response to a look from Duma: "It can wait."

A spark landed on Lucifer's arm unnoticed.

In the last five hours she'd filled a yellow legal notepad on the Eden events. Stray droplets of blood dotted the pad here and there, like ink drops from a broken pen.

Duma finally persuaded Maggie to let him change the dressing on her hands, and then he contented himself with pacing around the room.

Lucifer ran his hand through his short hair, changing it to a shoulder-length black that covered his face like a curtain. For the first time, Maggie noticed that Lucifer had hair. It seemed that these beings made a psychic impression. But unless you were looking at them, specific details seemed to fade into impressions only.

For the first time in a long, long while, Duma wished he had his wings back. A nighttime flight seemed very soothing right now. Duma had held Michael in an odd mix of disdain, for his pride and arrogance, and awe, for his discipline. But now it seemed one tragically overcame the other. Duma pretended to feel neither joy nor sadness at his death, but only shock.

Maggie replaced the poker in its iron holder and returned to her desk, where she went back to her pads and pen.

Honeybone stepped inside, uncharacteristically silent, his arms filled with a stack of firewood threatening to spill.

Duma moved to help him.

"How long's he been like that?" Honeybone whispered.

Nobody answered him.

"When are we going to bury the, uh, body?"

"In the morning," Lucifer said. "If that meets with your approval, Mr. Honeybone."

Honeybone stacked the wood against the wall. "At least somebody around here is getting buried."

A growl from the Lucifer. Duma stepped between

Honeybone and Lucifer. "You might consider keeping your commentary to yourself," Duma said. "These are most unusual circumstances."

Honeybone held his arms out. "And these aren't? Look at me. I'm a walking corpse. My wife used to joke that I worked too hard. I used to tell her I'd get plenty of rest when I was dead. Well, guess what? That isn't the fucking case. I'm chopping wood. So don't tell me about unusual circumstances, cause—"

"Andrew H. Honeybone, would you like to go to Hell—"

Honeybone snorted.

"And that is not a rhetorical question," Lucifer said.

"At least it would be an end."

"No, it would not be." Lucifer stood.

Duma pushed Honeybone to the front door. "Maybe you should collect more firewood."

"I don't think so." Honeybone pushed past Duma. "You pull me out of the lake, you hook one of your fucking claws into my gut, I get kidnapped and learn this is *not* a dream; that you've pulled my soul back into a rotting body so I can follow you around on some— you won't even let me see my wife. Fuck, I might be late to my own funeral and you sit there, Prince of the great whatever, moping because you killed an angel. At least you're alive, eh? At least you have choices."

Lucifer drew his hand back.

"That's it big man, go ahead, put me out of my misery or send me wherever. I don't care. So *growl* or lash out or whatever limited reaction it is that you have to things. You're like a child. A *child*. I don't have the Book. Michael didn't have the book. He was going to release me, release my *neshama* so that I can move on instead of being stuck in this rotting carcass. You didn't have to do what you did."

A long moment.

The air thickened.

Maggie found she could not draw a breath.

Duma's eyes glazed with emotion.

And finally.

"Yes, I did." And then Lucifer explained his deal with Yeshundra.

Honeybone spit a wet chunk of his tongue at Lucifer's feet. "I hate you."

Suddenly, Andrew Honeybone was pinned against the wall.

Maggie gasped. Duma took a step forward and stopped, not sure what to do.

"You have made your point, Mr. Honeybone," Lucifer said. "But you are not the only one in this cabin with..." He released his grip. Honeybone started to slide, but Lucifer helped him gently to his feet. "Busy yourself. My temper right now..."

Maggie spoke up. "I've got some tools in the shed, Andy. We could start on a casket. If that's okay with you, Lucifer. It would be something simple. Wooden."

"Maggie McCreedy, that would be an excellent idea."

"Come on, Honeybone," Maggie said. "Let's put some calluses on those hands."

"Yeah, okay." He straightened out his clothes. "I made a doghouse once."

Maggie threw on her coat, pulled a cigar from her pocket and lit up as she escorted Honeybone outside.

∞

"I've got a couple of things for you," Maggie said.

They sat in the barn, using old tree stumps for stools. Maggie lit up and instead of handing Honeybone a cigar, she handed him a roll of gauze.

He took it without saying a thing and wrapped the tan gauze around his bare and terrible abdomen. "I can hardly feel a thing."

She then handed him a gift, the book from the Wellspring.

He took it. "*The Law of Heaven*. Hmmph." Pause. "Thank you." He rubbed his wrists and ankles. "They never hung Christ upside down, did they?"

"Peter was crucified upside down," Maggie said. "In

humility to Christ."

"Never an innovator was Andrew Honeybone," he said in a stoic voice and then laughed to himself. He touched the remains of his right eye. "'Apologize, apologize, pluck out his eyes.'" He adjusted a makeshift eye patch. "I always had horrible vision. Started wearing glasses in the fourth grade. They made me look smart," he said. "That was the consensus-- thus dooming me to a barren romantic life. Rather the swashbuckling figure now, don't you think? Maybe I could be the model for the cover of your next book."

Maggie nodded, and blew out a ring of smoke. "Is that a wedding band?"

"I showed them," Honeybone said, tugging at it. It refused to slide off of his swollen finger. "Couldn't get rid of it if I wanted to. But there was a time..."

He leaned back stretching his arms, listening to the joints creak and crack as he wind-milled them slowly. "I suppose if this were a movie I would ask you if you thought we were going to get out of this alive." He craned his neck to look at the vaulted and shadowy ceiling of the barn.

"You said there was a time," Maggie said.

He looked at her, then back to his ring. Shook his head slowly in disbelief.

"Trouble with your marriage?"

"I hope not. I bought her a handgun for Christmas last

year," he said, laughingly. Then he quieted, a sobering expression on his face. "No trouble that she knew of."

"She...?"

"Julianne Grace, my wife." He let the last words linger, full of pride. "I named my boat after her. *Grace.*"

"And what was the trouble?"

"I kissed another woman."

Maggie nodded, biting her lip to keep from laughing. *"Kissed?"* She paused, waiting for him to say more. He glanced at the pad and pen on her lap. She set it down and he nodded in response.

"Sounds silly, doesn't it? Men cheating on their wives with prostitutes, best friends' sisters, daughters, and other men. And yes, I *kissed* another woman."

"We all fall to temptation. Don't you realize where we just came from?"

He waved his hand, dismissing her point. "I can't relate to that."

She nodded, chewing on her cigar. Then coughed.

"That's a nasty cough."

"It's nothing."

"What, compared to this," he said, indicating his body. "Then I concur."

"Cancer took both my breasts," she said. "The occasional cigar is going to have to work awfully hard to top that." She tapped the cigar and a sprinkle of ashes floated in the darkness.

"And your husband, during your battle?" Honeybone said.

"Harold was my rock. Stubborn son of a bitch," Maggie said. "Passed away a year ago. Massive heart attack. I held him in my arms as he died."

A few minutes of silence passed, punctuated only by Maggie's puffing and the useless labored breathing of someone breathing not from necessity, but out of habit.

"My wife is the most..." he struggled for a word, became frustrated that it did not come easily. "Spectacular woman I have ever met. Harold was your rock. Julianne was— *is* my angel in white. Pure as new snow, silver hair, rose colored eyes, alabaster skin, lips pale."

"Sounds like Snow White."

"Literally. She is an albino. We don't know about the baby yet."

"Oh. Huh." And before Maggie could formulate a more thoughtful response, Honeybone asked her a question: "So what interesting questions or conversation have you had with our Man in Black? I have a few curious questions, not that it matters much in the state I'm in. I just want to see my wife one more time."

"I asked him a couple. Why does God permit babies and children to die? And he said that the souls of murderers, killers and rapists and the like are sent back to earth in newborns so that they can experience as a pure vulnerable child the horror that they've inflicted on others as they die. That's why God lets children die. It's a punishment."

She took a drag on a cigar and coughed. "I mostly quit asking questions after that." Took another drag. "So, an albino?"

∞

Lucifer sank in the chair, picking at its wooden arm with a black fingernail. Splinters jumped and littered the floor at his feet.

Duma stopped his pacing and sat across the room from him.

"I have conducted battles, wars, skirmishes. I have ended them. I have rendered the belly of my brethren's wives, sisters and daughters barren as I raped them. I have decorated the Road to the Seventh Circle with the heads of babies. I do not punish those that do not deserve it, I do not punish those that do not ask for it. The one thing about death, Little One, is the ultimate knowledge of right and wrong." He paused. "Our rotting companion notwithstanding."

"I sense there is something else," Duma said. "Your mood since Eden has been most different, and if I may say, introspective."

"I overheard the writer use the word 'pouting.' I have lead rebellions. The greatest in Creation-- but I have never killed an archangel. I seem to be filled with guilt and, I believe, *remorse*, Little One."

"I am surprised at that," Duma said.

"I took that from another which I coveted."

"Forgive my ignorance."

"Little One, I did not only cease the existence of a Throne angel, but I took from him that which I so desperately seek."

"Oh?"

"Our instructions were clear, were they not? Destroy the thief, destroy those that stand in our way and we would be granted a wish. Does it not seem odd to you, Little One, that the Prince of Hell would subject himself to such bargaining, to such a game?"

"Well, yes, what could be granted that you could not grant yourself?"

"Exactly. After all, I rebelled against the Presence," Morning Star said. "And was rewarded with a kingdom, a third of the Host. Yes, what could I want?"

"I can think only to reclaim your position alongside the Lord. But how that relates to Michael--"

"I am ancient, I am tired, Little One. It is time for me to come to rest. I understand Honeybone's temper, his dilemma. All things come to an end, Little One. And the time for my end draws near. But I do not wish to die in my hellish palace. I wish to enter the Silver City, walk on its streets and lay in the Field of Gold with impunity and die there. "In short, Little One, my wish is to come home to die."

Maggie came into the cabin and stubbed out her cigar. "I got him working with the band-saw. The vibrations aren't doing his skin any good, though. I'm going to go back out there in a moment and relieve him. Need to get myself another Thermos of coffee."

"Thank you, Maggie," Morning Star said.

"Look, I hope this is okay," Maggie McCreedy said. "The casket will be stout and simple. Kind of fitting for the burial, I reckon."

"Mika'il was an archangel," Duma said.

"The burial will be far from simple," Lucifer said.

"I'm not quite sure I know what you mean," Maggie said, refilling her Thermos. "But in any case, one of you winged folks might want to think of a eulogy."

NINETEEN: *THE WAKE*

THE FOLLOWING MORNING, Margaret McCreedy's ranch saw a gathering unlike any the earth had ever seen.

> *There is an ongoing debate between scholars and men of the cloth as to the exact number of angels and demons. Fourteeth-century cabalists calculated the number to be 301,655,722. Albert Magnus tallied each choir at 6,666 legions, and each legion at 6,666, but although the number of the angels are fixed, the demons are capable of reproducing on their own. The Fallen were estimated in the 15th century by the Cardinal Bishop of Tusculum to be 133,306,668.*

*The number of the archangels from Geonic Lore
to Christian Gnostics to the testament of Solomon
to Talismanic Magic number is the same, though
actual names vary. The number is seven."*

—*Gustav Davidson*

A Dictionary of Angels

Until now.

Duma wandered out to the front porch at the first signs of a graying sky. Maggie was already there, sipping coffee from a ceramic mug with the logo BLUE SAPPHIRE.

"I buried my husband out there," she said. "Actually, I scattered his ashes."

"It is a beautiful place. I would love to walk it someday. It resembles the Southern Slope of Heaven," Duma said. "If you squint."

Maggie nodded and then Duma pounded his fist on the railing, cracking the wood.

He looked down in disbelief at what he had done. Turning his fist over, he slowly picked out a long splinter. "I am sorry."

"Nothing that can't be fixed," Maggie said. "Harold used to take it out on the woodpile. Always had more than enough firewood. Who are you angry at?"

"Myself, my ambivalence." He sighed. "And you, how

do you feel?"

She sipped her coffee. "I feel like I'm just along for the ride."

"I doubt that."

"I slept pretty good all things considered."

"Where is Honeybone?"

"In the barn, finishing the coffin."

As if on cue, Honeybone stepped from the barn, and lumbered up to the front porch. "Done."

"Let's bring the body out for the wake," Duma said.

"The wake?" Honeybone said, incredulously. "We're having a wake? Nobody—"

"It's more of a viewing," Duma said. "Lucifer said to bring the body to the porch and wait for him."

"It's never done, is it?" Honeybone said.

∞

They placed the body of Mika'il on a long table Maggie's husband had made so many years ago, and brought it out to the front porch. It was laid out carefully, shrouded with a simple linen sheet. Maggie put a rose in its hands.

Lucifer stepped out, dressed in black, his head now dark and smooth. He pricked one of his fingers and traced Michael's sigil on the body's chest.

Duma sat perched on the railing and stared blankly at the body. His wings hung down his back, crooked and useless.

"He sure smells like lilacs," Honeybone said. "It's getting stronger."

"Wish I could say the same about you," Maggie said, with a good-natured smile as she reached for a cigar. She struck a match along the railing and paused. "You smell that?"

"Smell what, the lilacs?"

"No, something else."

"Hey," Honeybone said. "What happened to the sun?" He squinted through a gray hand. The sun disappeared behind a swirling black cloud, which moved toward them, although there was no breeze. The temperature dropped several degrees.

"Rotting wood," Maggie said. The match burned the tip of Maggie's finger, and she dropped it. "I smell rotting wood."

"Yes," Duma said. "*They* are coming."

"Who's coming?" Honeybone said.

"The Fallen."

The swirling cloud pulsed with a life of its own, like a school of fish; individual figures broke from the school and circled overhead.

To Maggie they looked like tiny birds—

No, bats...

A score more joined the ones that had broken apart, and soon their flight took the shape of a thick ellipse, painting a black halo around the cabin. The smell grew.

Duma shifted nervously, trying in vain to recognize a face.

Honeybone craned his neck. "Those are the Fallen, huh? Well, I'm glad you're with us, Lucifer."

"I am afraid I cannot guarantee your safety."

"Great," Honeybone said. "If I had functioning bowels, I'd be shitting myself."

A dozen bats twittered and screeched and broke loose from the spinning halo; they spiraled down a good fifty yards from the porch and disappeared into the woods. They blurred and shifted into one as they disappeared. Moments later, a figure emerged on the path, wings tucked in tightly behind as it strode forward.

Honeybone took a few steps up the porch and stood slightly behind Maggie. Duma arched his wings, flexing them to their fullest, and slowly closed them. The effort was a poor display, resembling the branches of a weeping willow.

The figure wore a black tunic with a silver symbol. He bowed towards the group. "Margaret McCreedy, the witness; Andrew Honeybone, the deceased; Duma, the Little Rebel—"

Duma snapped off the rest of the railing. He raised it in an offensive gesture.

The figure raised his hand, palm open. "I mean that as a compliment."

Duma lowered the piece of wood, but did not drop it.

"So ends the first Archangel." The figure now addressed Lucifer who walked to the edge of the porch and looked down. "Milord, you do not cease to surprise me. It appears your request has met with a most interesting twist."

"Yes, Verrier, it appears so," Lucifer sad, guardedly. "How are things in my Kingdom?"

"Nasty rumors," Verrier said. "Are circulating that you have betrayed your crown, Milord."

"And where stand you, Verrier?"

"Loyal to the crown prince, of course. But the dukes and other princes are readying themselves for war. A number of them are claiming to be the new *ha-satan*. I believe they were intending to take the First Great Spire by force, but this…" He gestured towards the body of Michael. "Has been a cause for a celebration not seen since the Fall. And rather unexpected considering—" He eyed the humans. "Our talk before your departure." He paused. "Is it to be, or have the plans changed?"

"Are they coming down?" Lucifer looked skyward.

"I see," Verrier said. His nostrils flared. "Yes."

The sky to the east grew bright as a white cloud

formed and blew in, oblivious to any jet stream. Soon a band formed, pulsing with golden wings and ivory bodies. They formed another halo, this one above the black one; slowly it lowered to form a concentric ring, which in turn expanded until the halo became one mass of vibrating gray.

Slowly, like snowflakes, a mix of black and gold feathers drifted to the ground. Verrier picked up a golden one and a black one. Handed them to Maggie. "For the scribe."

Maggie took them with hesitation. She stroked both of them. The golden one was coarse and prickly, the black one smoother than silk. She tucked them both into her front shirt pocket and turned her attention back to the source of the feather fall.

The rings separated: one white, one dark, moving in vertical circles like the sides of a Ferris wheel. Five figures broke from the white ring and landed. Both rings continued to circle for a minute, and then broke symmetry, pouring down. The white band spiraled slowly to a graceful, almost choreographed landing; the dark without rhyme or reason, each creature at its own speed and style. The five figures made their way to the porch. Two of them had trouble walking and two others trying to keep them on their feet. One walked straight up to body of Michael.

Maggie glanced at Duma.

"The Archangels," Duma whispered.

The two stronger archangels fell at the body of Michael and wept uncontrollably with their brothers. The remaining one did not.

"Morning, Uriel."

"Yes, Light Giver, it is a day of Mourning," Uriel said. "And it shall become an evening of reckoning."

"I empathize with you, Brother," Lucifer said. "My heart—"

"LIES, Morning Star. Your lies will end. I will see you wiped from Creation. I will not rest until—"

"You echo Mika'il's last words," Lucifer said.

"*Please,* Uriel," Duma intervened. "Some decorum, please. The Light Giver was instructed by the Presence to—"

"First Cassiel and now Mika'il?" Verrier commented. "Oh, you have grown up."

"So you have finally Fallen, *He Who Walks*," Uriel said. "And in what a grand way, Little Rebel." His wings extended; Duma's flexed, exciting little more than a twitch.

Duma lunged at Uriel, but Lucifer's hand snagged the little angel out of midair and set him gently on the porch. "If you would take a moment, you would notice that Duma's wings are the color of yours. They have not turned, nor has he Fallen. You had better recognize the significance of that."

Duma shrugged off Lucifer's hand. He climbed to the

top of the cabin and perched on the edge of its roof like a gargoyle.

"Where is Ramiel?"

"Missing and suspect along with the Sopheriel twins," Uriel said.

"Let us not forget our manners, Archangel," Verrier said. "We are here for mourning."

Uriel's wings flittered, kicking up a small spiral of leaves.

"Let the viewing begin," Lucifer said, solemnly.

And they began to file past the body of The Archangel Mika'il.

∞

The pungent aroma of rotting wood, mixed with that of lilacs, grew so thick that Maggie had to hold her handkerchief to her face for a moment. Long enough for a few of the Fallen to file past. Some faces leaked secret smiles; some filed past with damp cheeks. Others still walked past and touched the body. More than a few, though, eyed Lucifer with suspicion.

One remarked to Duma, "So, Little Rebel, will you become the Sixth or Seventh?"

"You should have Fallen..."

"But he did bring the rebellion home, did he not?"

Duma sat silently, his face twitching with recognition at some of the faces, blank at others, all the while lightly scratching a shingle. One held his gaze.

A one-eyed Host angel.

"Man, and I thought I smelled bad," Honeybone said.

Just then the distant sound of an engine reached Maggie's ears. At the front gate was a beat-up pickup. She nudged Honeybone, who in turn shrugged. "I thought everyone who was anyone was here."

She looked at Lucifer, who followed her gaze. He nodded to her. "Don't stray too far."

Maggie stepped into the cabin and returned a moment later with a shotgun. She cradled it in the crook of her right arm, and headed for the gate.

Honeybone followed. "I bet those birds don't take too kindly to that boomstick of yours."

"It's not for anything with a beak, if you know what I mean."

The man at the gate had hopped up on the hood of his truck and sat idly kicking his legs. Next to him was a well-used rucksack. When Maggie and Honeybone got to the gate, he slid off and smiled. "Hello."

"I'm sorry this is private property," Maggie said.

"So I've read," he said, indicating the weathered signs on the gate.

He was a tall, lean man dressed in cowboy casual, a

sports jacket over an open collar denim shirt. His blue jeans were faded and almost too comfortable looking, with a few threadbare spots around the pockets and knees. The cuffs of the jeans were pulled down over snakeskin boots which were caked with mud and straw. A simple brown leather belt circled his waist like a flat snake.

His face was gaunt and clean shaven, but not without humor. He smiled, and deep lines formed from the corner of his eyes. His hair was graying and slicked back into a ponytail, which revealed itself when he retrieved his bag from the truck.

"I'd be a little slower with your movements, fellow," Maggie said, almost casually pumping the shotgun. She reminded him of one or two characters that inhabited her novel from time to time.

"I understand," he said, slowly reaching into his sack. He produced a plain looking envelope and handed it to Maggie with two fingers. "Open it."

She did. And pulled out a linen invitation with simple gold script:

YOUR PRESENCE IS NOW REQUESTED
AT THE MCCREEDY RANCH

"Where'd you get this?" Maggie said, noticing for the first time the two feathers attached to the ponytail band.

"Who the hell are you?"

"James Kirkland, I'm here to lead the sermon."

"Who sent you?"

He laughed. "Who do you think?"

And then his eyes narrowed, focused past Maggie.

She turned.

"I'd hoped to get here before they did." He took out a small leather bag, opened it, licked his finger and stuck it into the bag. He pulled it out, a gray ash coating his finger. He traced a circle on his forehead, dipped the finger again and looked at Maggie. "You might want to do the same."

"What's in the bag?"

"Ashes."

"What kind?"

"The gray kind."

"Nothing special about it?"

"Not yet."

"I would advise you do the same as me," he said to Honeybone. "Dead or not dead."

Now Maggie's eyes narrowed. "You're that fella from the Wellspring. In the back room."

"Yes." Kirkland stepped forward and slowly traced a circle on her forehead. "I look different after a good shave."

"That's not the mark of the beast, is it?" Honeybone asked, half seriously.

"That's not a bad question, Mr. Honeybone. It isn't, I assure you."

"Okay," Honeybone said, and leaned forward to receive the mark.

"Now let's hold hands in a circle. And bow our heads."

They did so, and Kirkland began to speak in what sounded like a mix of Hebrew and Greek. She felt a burning sensation on her forehead, and tried to jerk her hand away, but Kirkland held fast. She pulled harder. She opened her eyes and his head was still bent, still speaking in tongues.

Thirty seconds passed, and the burning intensified.

Honeybone was silent.

Maggie opened her mouth to say something in protest, and found she couldn't articulate anything.

And then it was gone.

Kirkland loosened his grip on her hand. She stumbled back, tripping over the shotgun. She grabbed it in a panic, and it discharged, catching Honeybone in the shoulder. He spun around and fell to the ground.

"Hey!" Honeybone exclaimed. "Cut it out." He looked at his shoulder. Four dime-sized holes adorned his shirt. "You're going to have to dig them out."

"I— I'm sorry, Andy," Maggie stammered. She pushed herself to her feet. "But my head..."

The circle on Kirkland's head was no longer a rough ash shape but a thin silver circle similar to the one on Mr. Pouge's forehead.

She touched her forehead. Could actually feel the warm ring. "What?"

"Some still call it the mark of Cain. It's merely a warning to the Host and Fallen. Do not harm those with the mark— or face the wrath of the Lord."

"Well, I certainly feel better," Honeybone said, not without a trace of sarcasm.

"If it's okay with you I'd like to grab a quick shower and change before the service," Kirkland said.

Maggie nodded and unlocked the gate, and together, they drove up to the cabin.

"Whereabouts you from, mister?"

"New York," he said. "Originally."

TWENTY: *THE WOODS*

JIMMY, as James Kirkland told the group to call him, rubbed his wet hair with a towel and kicked his bare feet up on the table. "Long drive," he muttered to himself.

"We'll have to get up early to dig it," Maggie said. "Jimmy, I hope you brought your gloves."

"The grave is already dug," Duma said. "Each of the Fallen and Host scooped a handful of dirt as they passed the chosen grave site." He stood at the window and gazed out. His lips twitched, and it was obvious he was talking to himself. He still clutched the piece of wood he had from earlier that morning. "It is our way."

Lucifer sat on the porch, with Honeybone at the other end.

The Host angels and Fallen were not to be seen.

"They out there?" Maggie said, setting a cup of coffee on the table by Kirkland.

"Thanks," Jimmy said.

"The Host have probably taken flight," Duma said. "It's a weekly ritual."

"You going to join them?"

Duma gave her a look.

"That's a damn fine cup of coffee, Maggie," Jimmy said. "But I was hoping you might have something else to freshen it up a bit." He scooted the cup towards her. "If you don't mind."

She went to her writing desk and pulled out a bottle of scotch. "One shot or two?"

He thought about it for a second and then raised two fingers.

She poured it into his coffee cup with a wink. "Mind if I join you?"

"Please do so."

"I'm going for a walk," Duma said, and abruptly left.

"So, Maggie McCreedy," Jimmy said, looking at the bookshelves. "Seems you're quite the storyteller."

"I've told a yarn or two."

He nodded. "So how'd you get this gig? I don't imagine your agent turned you onto it." He nodded at her stack of yellow notepads. *"The First Book of Margaret?"*

She chuckled and downed a shot without the coffee.

"I've got a few titles. That one sounds a little pretentious. I need an ending first."

"I imagine it'll come to you in big bold letters." He scribbled some notes of his own. "I only wish the sermon would come as easily. Of course, look who I'll be preaching to."

Maggie laughed. "Maybe you should just keep it simple."

"I think you're right."

"How long have you been a priest?" Maggie asked.

"I *used* to be a priest."

"Why'd you quit?"

"Why'd *you* quit?"

She gave it some thought. Sipped her coffee. "I looked back on my life these last few months after my husband's death, and realized I hadn't said anything important." Maggie paused. "I hope that's not the case for you."

"I'm what they call a priest fallen from grace. A few accusations here and there, an overly zealous parent with the worst of suspicions. It was a battle that couldn't be won. I had plenty of support, but once some of those news crews roll tape. Words like 'alleged,' 'suspected of' are just synonyms for guilty."

"So what are you doing now?"

"Research. For various people: mostly biblical, historical, theological, archeology, geology, physics, quantum mechanics. God is a mathematician, you know." He took a sip. "I'm currently researching a book excised from the Bible. It expands on the Nephilim and sons of God. Guess the Church didn't want that one floating around."

"Sounds intriguing," Maggie said.

"The stuff I've learned," Kirkland said. "It's opened my heart and mind like nothing else. I'm actually thinking about teaching."

"I bet you'd make a great teacher."

"Try me. Ask me a question."

"How did God create everything in six days?"

"That's an easy one." He picked up a pencil and tore a blank sheet out of Maggie's note pad.

A shriek pierced the night.

"The hell?"

"Exactly," Jimmy said, pulling on his jeans.

Maggie spilled her coffee as she grabbed her shotgun. Kirkland reached into his rucksack and pulled out a pearl-handled Colt revolver.

They rushed outside. Lucifer stepped off the porch and stared intently into the woods.

"Did you hear that?" Maggie said, ignoring the pain it took to ratchet a shell. "I've never heard anything like that."

"Yes," Lucifer said, grimly. "You have."

"I dare guess," Jimmy said. "That was the scream of an

angel."

"Did Duma come back?"

The scream again.

"There," Lucifer said, pointing to the path veering off to the left. The sun had dipped below the horizon and light was fading. The trio dashed off, and soon came to the crossroads.

"Which way?"

Maggie stopped and strained to hear something, anything but the pounding of her heart and the wheezing of her lungs.

Lucifer held up his hand, and Maggie held her breath. Kirkland pointed his Colt down the path to the right.

"That way," he said, and was gone.

Maggie charged after him. On the run she glanced behind her, and Lucifer was gone.

Jimmy Kirkland disappeared around the bend.

Another scream.

This one was cut short. Maggie stumbled and then fell to the ground. She lay there for a moment just wanting it to end. But as always something gave her a swift kick—

Not here, not now, cowgirl...

—and she climbed to her feet. Her ankle flared with pain, but she ignored it, hurrying as fast as she could.

She entered the clearing on the path as Jimmy brought his weapon to bear.

"In the name of Christ, I command you to stop!"

Maggie's forehead burned as she noticed the target of Jimmy's weapon.

At the far side of the clearing, two Fallen sat hunched over two bodies. The first she recognized as Duma, face down. One of his wings was bent back on itself in several places; the other was precariously attached by a few thin ropes of tendons, muscle and sinew.

The other body, she thought, was Honeybone.

The Fallen ripped Duma's wing from its socket and held the bloody nub to its mouth.

Angel blood poured into and overflowed its maw. Maggie could hear the uncouth gulping noises it made. She raised her shotgun.

Jimmy fired first.

The Fallen by Honeybone took a bullet in the chest, dropping a loop of intestine snaking down to a gray body partially hidden in the brush.

The second shrieked, more in anger than in pain. It stood its full height and spread its wings; its arms dropped to its sides and it took slow steps towards Jimmy.

"Maggie, get back!" Kirkland shouted with a voice lower and deeper than she imagined him capable of.

But ever stubborn, Maggie merely raised her gun and put a slug into the first Fallen's shoulder, knocking it off Duma. A snapping sound reached her ears.

She turned.

Several more Fallen attacked, leaves kicking up in the wind swirls of their wings.

They were surrounded.

Kirkland rushed to her. Instinctively they turned back to back, and without a word they began to fire as the starlit sky filled with bats and Fallen.

The battle, though valiant, lasted but seconds.

A trio, led by Verrier, dragged Jimmy away from Maggie and began to torture him, poking holes in his flesh with their claws. "I have the mark," Jimmy spat through a bubble of blood.

"Yes," Verrier said, and with his forefinger claw cut the mark from his forehead. "You *had* the mark." Another Fallen dragged Maggie over to Jimmy, forced her to her knees and made her watch.

"Open your mouth, monkey," Verrier said.

A Fallen forced open her mouth as Verrier placed the bloody piece of flesh on her tongue.

"VER-RI-ER!"

They all froze.

The Morning Star formed in the center of the clearing. "These children have the *mark*. And right now *I* am in *His* service."

Verrier stood. "You cannot reign and serve at the same time, Light Giver. You have betrayed your own. You cannot hide it from me, like you have these monkeys."

"You know not of what you speak," Lucifer said. "You are clumsy and stupid, despite your rank."

"Which will be *ha-satan*, soon," Verrier said. "You have no intentions of fulfilling the plans for the Second Rebellion."

Lucifer raised his wings high and smashed them to the ground. White light emanated from him like a blast, knocking all the Fallen to their feet. The remaining leaves on the trees flittered to the ground, blackened.

Verrier staggered on his feet, punch drunk.

"You forget who I am," Lucifer said. "Not only the First of the Fallen, but the First Formed. In the beginning, as you had six wings, I soared with twelve. I wore the other angels as a garment, transcending all in glory and knowledge. I am the Light Giver, the Light Bringer, the evening star, the morning star. I am *Sammael,* who tempted Lilith, who seduced Eve and became by her the father of Cain. *Behold the Lord's Brightest Child.*"

D.S. Hay

Light

And nothing more...

Then the still air filled with inhuman shrieks of pain and terror.

Maggie opened her eyes. Verrier stood, the feathers burned off his wings and his eyes a blackened mess. The other Fallen lay charred and smoldering. She looked at Jimmy. His chest rose and fell slowly, erratically. She spit out the flesh, crawled over to him and cradled his head, resting it gently on her lap; blood from his head wound quickly soaked her handkerchief, but she continued to dab softly at it, humming some long forgotten lullaby.

And then Verrier opened his eyes. "I expected more, toad." He grabbed Maggie by the hair and extended his claws under the softness of her neck. And Maggie knew her time was at an end.

"This is your witness, yes?" Verrier said to no one and everyone. "The one who will reconcile your history, as predicted by those monkeys Jerome, Gregory of Nyssa, Origen and Ambrosiaster—"

He stopped speaking. His head lolled forward and he sank to his knees. Duma stood behind him, the piece of splintered railing clutched with both hands dripping black. "I am Duma, once Jophiel, now He Who Walks." He spun Verrier around. "And I am of the Host."

He plunged his hand into Verrier's chest and pulled out his onyx heart. Gore ran from between his fingers as he squeezed the heart to pulp.

Silence filled the woods for a long heartbeat.

"A little help, please..." It was Honeybone, still down, his intestines looping around his legs and nearby trees.

The makeshift stake slipped from Duma's hands and he staggered over to Honeybone.

Jimmy's arm moved slowly. His fingers laced with Maggie's. She squeezed them gently and wrung his blood from the rag with her other hand. She dabbed the blood from his eyes, and they opened, crossed, and then slowly focused on her. The corner of his mouth twitched; air escaped from his lips as a coughing spasm wracked his body. His grip tightened on her arm.

"Jimmy, it's okay," Maggie said. "You're going to be okay."

This time, both corners of his mouth turned into a smile. The kind you would give a child who swears he hasn't gotten into the candy, but wears a mustache of chocolate.

"You're a good lass, Maggie McCreedy. God loves you."

Tears streamed down Maggie's face, mixing with Kirkland's blood.

Arms folded, Lucifer stood to the side, face stoic.

"Do it, Morning Star," Maggie said. "Save him."

"He is already saved."

"Save his physical body. Do it. I'll give you whatever you want."

"You want to make a deal?"

Kirkland's hand tightened. "Maggie, no."

"Whatever you want."

"I am disappointed with you, Maggie." And then he walked away.

A gathering of birds circled on the outside fringe of the woods.

Kirkland's eyes glazed over.

"Jimmy? Jimmy…?"

They focused. "You want me to take a message to Harry for you?"

"No, you're gonna be okay."

He hushed her with a finger. "The message…"

"I miss you every single day, you son of a bitch."

"I miss you too, Shorty. Come rain or shine."

Kirkland's body jolted as he laughed. Another wave of blood covered his face. He looked over her shoulder.

"It's… *beautiful…*"

∞

Maggie stood on the porch, her clothes covered with a brown mix of dried blood and dirt. Her hands ached, and the blisters weren't helping; she could barely hold the shovel. She shook out two painkillers, and poured herself two fingers of scotch. When she went to pop the pills, Lucifer's hand stopped hers.

"It was not within my power to save him."

"Lord's brightest child," she said, sarcastically and spat on his feet. "Turn me loose."

He did so, and the pain in her hands ceased. She looked at him. "You don't give two shits about us, do you? I mean, how could you. You've been around since day one—"

"Day three, actually."

"And you just don't give a shit about us. You didn't think twice about killing Michael. From what I read I thought you'd be a little more enlightened, but I guess that's not really in your nature, is it?"

"Why do you mourn for Kirkland, McCreedy? You only knew him for less than a day. Did you love him?"

"Are you so blind?"

"You would have given your soul to me for him to live. A stranger, a person who meant nothing to you."

"You are blind. Don't you see what he could have done with the rest of his life? He had years and years left to continue. To do important work, to spread salvation, understanding. I'm just an old romance writer"

"McCreedy, you call yourself a hack, because it comes so easy to you, as it does with most of the gifted."

He took a deep breath and sighed. "I rarely like to speak of the Plan. And although you are a very small piece of that Plan, there is no such thing as an unimportant piece."

"Sounds like the shit end of the stick to me," Honeybone said, toting another shovel from the barn. His stomach bulged from a new set of wrappings. "All those stink angels gone?" He looked at Lucifer. "No, I guess not. Where's Duma?"

"Off pouting, I reckon." She reached into her coveralls and tossed him a set of keys. "Andy, sweetie, do me a favor and bring Jimmy's truck up to the barn."

"Sure thing, boss."

"Shouldn't you be writing, scribe?"

Maggie wrung her hands, massaging them. They felt better than she could ever remember. And she hated him for it.

"After I bury Kirkland."

∞

The scotch and painkillers worked their magic as she began to dig a grave in the clearing. Despite the battle and the gore, the air seemed as clear as she ever remembered it. She shifted Jimmy's revolver to the other side of her jacket. The body lay next to the beginning of his grave. "Thank you, Jimmy," she said, and continued to dig, wishing she could ask him more questions.

Something moved to her left.

She yanked the pistol out of her pocket and cocked it.

"Maggie..." It was Jimmy.

She rubbed her eyes and looked around for a sign of a trick. But there was none.

Jimmy smiled with blood stained teeth. "I think reports of my death have been greatly exaggerated."

∞

Silence permeated the land. No birdsong, no symphony of crickets; no scratching of fallen leaves outside her window. Maggie sat back in her chair at her desk. Jimmy lay on the couch, his wounds dressed and healing rapidly. When she asked him what had happened he said, "They told me it wasn't my time yet." And then he passed out.

Maggie set down her pencil, rubbed her eyes and turned down the wick on her oil lamp. Three full legal pads sat on her desk.

∞

The shaking again.

A hand on her shoulder.

"Maggie?"

Maggie awoke. Rubbed her eyes. Six legal pads.

How?

"Maggie," Honeybone said. "It's time. We're going back to the Wellspring."

TWENTY-ONE: *THE WELLSPRING II*

THE AROMA TWEAKED Maggie's nose and made her stomach growl. Yeshundra had set a table for five. The table and chairs were handcrafted and elegant in their simplicity; Maggie assumed Yeshundra had made them, but was too embarrassed to ask.

Yeshundra entered from the small kitchen, carrying a platter of cheese and crackers. "I thought we'd start with an appetizer."

"And wine?" Duma said.

"I'm glad you asked." He then turned and went into another room. Through the doorway, Maggie could see him descend a set of wooden stairs. He returned a moment later, dirt smeared on his white T-shirt, and set two bottles on the table.

Maggie, not a connoisseur of wine, did not recognize the label.

Yeshundra opened both bottles with a simple corkscrew and set one on either end of the table. "We'll let them breathe for a minute."

Duma gasped, and slowly picked up one of the bottles. "From the Fields of Paradise," he said. "Home."

"The finest wine in Creation." Then he chuckled. "I'm sorry, Mrs. McCreedy. It must be something to hear, people speak so grandiose and literal at the same time."

"I'm getting used to it." She closed her eyes, and she could smell the wine. A faint honey scent, perhaps some lilac. "Wine from Heaven?"

"Exactly. The bottle in front of you is from the Western region; the other is from the Southern Slopes. I took a few bottles with me."

"How many?" Duma asked.

"Homesick already?" He poured Maggie a glass, and then Honeybone.

"After my first book sold," Maggie said. "I sent back a bottle of the good stuff. Didn't know what was wrong with it. Just sent it back because I could. Don't guess there's any cause for that now."

"Light Giver, would you care for a glass?" Yeshundra said.

"No."

"It's probably been a while."

"I remember the taste. There are a few things that stick with you for fifteen billion years."

"Is Hell but a taste of Heaven?" Kirkland said.

Maggie stifled a laugh.

Yeshundra smiled. "It's okay to laugh."

"The Book?" Lucifer said.

"In due time, Light Giver. Let us talk over wine, and after dinner we will get to the business of the Book. But now, fellowship."

"And a hell of an assortment at that," Honeybone said, peaking over his thick book.

Yeshundra laughed. Full and rich.

Without a care in the world, Maggie thought.

"So Mr. Honeybone, did you have such a sense of humor while you were alive?"

"Christ, no."

The room laughed.

Even Lucifer smiled. "Perhaps one glass."

∞

"Let's see, we have the Prince of Lies, a dead man talking, Jophiel the Penitent angel, and a woman," Yeshundra said. "And my good friend Mr. Kirkland."

Yeshundra pointed to Duma and nodded to Maggie.

"When he was known as Jophiel, he drove your parents out of Eden."

"Oh."

"Really," Honeybone said. "How do you respond to something like that?"

"I did as I was told," Duma said.

"You liked them, didn't you?"

"Yes," Duma said. "Humans have their— they remind me of angels. With their follies. I was saddened to escort them out, but also amazed at their progress. Really."

"Progress?" Honeybone said. "War, disease—"

"And you have survived that in spite of yourselves. The Seraphim and Cherubim would not have lasted. Lazy and prideful. Don't you agree, Lucifer?"

"Yes, Lucifer," Kirkland said. "Tell us your opinion."

Lucifer swirled the wine in his glass. "The wine is excellent."

"Can you tell from what vineyard?"

"He's testing me," Lucifer said. "Do you see that?"

Silence.

"There is no need, Yeshundra."

"And?"

"I am Sammael, Lucifer Morning Star, Light Giver, et al."

"Just making sure," Yeshundra said. "I don't see you folks too often."

"I don't follow," Maggie said.

"Satan is an office," Yeshundra said, sipping his wine. "It's Hebrew for the 'adversary.' Historically the fallen angel Lucifer has been identified as being Satan. But they are two separate entities. But fifteen billion years is a long time to hold the Throne. How many have held the Throne?"

"I am the first and the sixth," Lucifer said. "Semyaza before me and Olivier before him."

"One of the Seraphim and one of the order of Archangels."

"You guys have term limits," Honeybone said. "Or elections or what?"

"Olivier's head is on a pike outside the Palace of the Fifth Circle."

"So how are things in hell?"

"Many factions of infighting still. The dukes fancy themselves princes; the princes, kings. The souls of the damned are still surprised at how unoriginal their sins are. Souls begging to be tortured for crimes long forgotten, the victims' and the criminals' genealogy long since petered out. But there are parts of Hell that are still quite beautiful. In some places you would actually think you were in Heaven," Lucifer sighed. "But the wine there, I now realize, is quite lacking."

"Fitting, don't you suppose?" Yeshundra stretched and

yawned. "So, Andrew Lazarus. You seem quite uncomfortable."

"No offense, but my butt is rotting off. I thought maybe you guys might be able to do something about that. The rotting. I figure I can get the leper discount."

Yeshundra laughed.

"May I take a look at your knife, Morning Star?" Kirkland said. "I've had quite a collection in my time."

Lucifer untied the sheath from his belt and handed it hilt first to Kirkland. "Be careful. That blade can cleave the oxygen molecule from its hydrogen neighbors."

The table laughed, but none doubted that it could.

"Will do," Kirkland said. He settled back in his chair and carefully drew the blade and began studying the ever-changing etchings on the blade.

"If I'm not mistaken," Yeshundra said, glancing over. "The blade contains elements of the Presence, and things which are to pass and perhaps not to pass."

"What do you mean?"

"There is an Alpha and Omega, a beginning and an end. But the points between, the paths we travel, are not so clear. As I'm sure you all have experienced."

"What is this?" Kirkland said, indicating a spot on the blade.

Yeshundra looked at it. "The creation of the first angel, the Morning Star."

"And this one?"

Yeshundra leaned forward, and Kirkland drove the blade into his chest.

"KIRKLAND!" Maggie screamed.

Blood seeped from the wound and ran down the blade's blood groove.

"What the—"

Yeshundra's hands grasped for the blade as his eyes went wide.

Kirkland torqued the knife, twisting open flesh. "Die, Yeshundra, die, Son of Mary."

Duma bolted across the table and Kirkland swung an open hand, catching the misfit angel across the neck and sending him flying into Honeybone.

Lucifer lithely dodged the sprawling angel and lawyer, clearing the table with a single bound. With a clawed hand he grabbed Kirkland by the neck, pulled him off Yeshundra and pinned him to the wall.

Maggie rushed over to Yeshundra, who swayed for a moment. She offered him as much support as she could. A tear ran from his eye.

"My Lord," Maggie said. "What can I do?"

"Hold my hand, Margaret McCreedy."

"Take my life, if it will help you, my Lord."

He squeezed her hand. "You would do that for me, Maggie?"

"Yes."

"Yes, you would, wouldn't you?" He smiled sweetly. "And in return?"

She lowered her head.

"Nothing?" He touched her cheek with a bloodied hand. With the other he slowly withdrew the blade. The blood soaked into the metal, disappearing completely. He stood erect, lifting Maggie's chin.

"You have a productive life ahead of you, Maggie. I can only hope you will find the peace you need."

Kirkland let out an unearthly scream, flailing like an insect pinned to the wall.

Lucifer matched the scream with a lion's roar of his own and silenced Kirkland; he drew back a hooked hand and shoved his fist down the priest's throat.

Kirkland squirmed.

Maggie heard Honeybone gasp.

"What's he doing to Kirkland?"

"That's not Kirkland," Duma said. "But I'm not sure which one it is."

"Which one?" Maggie said.

Lucifer withdrew his hand violently as if removing a hook from a fish. Kirkland's flesh shuddered and collapsed like a heavy drape around a wet and glistening scaled body. Lucifer threw the body to the ground. It thudded with a wet, sickening sound.

Yeshundra stepped up to the body, his wounds closing as he did. "The ignorance of the Fallen. It never ceases to amaze me." He bent down and touched the demon's lips. "I forgive you."

The demon spit black bile in Yeshundra's face.

Lucifer thrust his hand into the demon's mouth and started to pinch off its black tongue.

"Wait," Duma said. "It is *Verrier.*"

Lucifer withdrew his hand, and instead broke both the demon's legs.

Maggie looked at the heap of Kirkland flesh. "What happened to Jimmy?"

"Kirkland is dead, killed at the battle in the woods. Verrier possessed his flesh. His soul is with Him, though."

Verrier coughed up a tar-like substance. It dripped slowly from his purple lips. "You all are doomed. The Omega will not happen. Yeshundra, Son of God, don't you see it? The Heavenly *beth din* is corrupt. The Sopheriel twins knew it and took the Book of Life."

"You forget *I* am the Lord of Lies," Lucifer said.

"We have never forgotten that, Star of the Morning." Verrier said. "But what I say comes from Sopheriel mouths."

"What?"

"Sopheriel Memeth has been captured and tortured in Hell. By my order. He tried to be strong, but he has grown soft, so very soft, like the underbelly of a newborn. I think he enjoyed telling us. His body seemed to be filled with relief. We ceased torturing him after that, since angels cannot lie directly, especially those so strong with the Presence like the Judgment Twins."

Duma spoke: "I cannot conceive of you showing Mercy. Not after the woods, not after here."

"I showed him no Mercy, Little Rebel. It is simply because his news was so great that I had more important matters to attend."

Duma stepped up to him, but said nothing. Lucifer adjusted his grip on Verrier's neck.

"You don't know, do you?"

Silence.

"There was a conspiracy to rid Heaven of Michael the Destroyer. A conspiracy with roots in the Council. You should be happy, Duma. Did he not sit in judgment of you in the Cassiel trial? Was it not he who recommended the rack?"

Duma turned away.

"Conspiracy?" Maggie said. "Why would they want to rid Heaven of Michael?"

"To pave the way for the Second Rebellion, isn't that right, Light Giver?"

A creature flittered at the windowsill. Lucifer turned its way, and Verrier went slack in his grip, inert and lifeless.

"The bat!" Lucifer exclaimed. But it was too late. Maggie looked out the window, and the bat had joined hundreds of others, becoming lost among its brothers.

"Should have broken its neck," Duma said.

"I don't completely understand this conspiracy. Who started it?"

"There is no conspiracy," Lucifer said, strongly. "That is not possible."

Duma said nothing.

"We need to rescue Sopheriel Memeth," Maggie said.

"Let him rot," Duma said.

"He's your brother," Maggie said.

"Like Michael?" Duma said, sternly.

Honeybone leaned on the table. "You guys are giving me a headache. I die and make it just to the edge of Heaven, or some bright light, and I get yanked back. Sure, I was surprised, and I had a few regrets— a *few*, mind you. I never learned to snow ski and maybe at times I wasn't the best husband I could have been, but I was willing to follow the rules despite that. As a lawyer— a damn good one, I made a difference in some lives. And that was good enough for me. I was ready to go and you guys in your little cosmic chess game had to pull me here and for what reason?"

He swatted the bottles of wine off the table. They shattered against the floor.

"So you could prance and pose and posture and talk in

butchered Elizabethan of alpha and omega and the gates of Heaven and the key to Hell and who makes the best wine. What about me and my selfish little soul, huh? I'm stinking here! And Maggie, you couldn't be happy with writing romance books. This 'angel' killed your *brother* to further his own means. Your own brother. Are you going to disown him in death? Trust me. I learned a few things hanging by my feet from that tree. This 'prince' will stop at nothing if it furthers *his* ends. No one else's. And you…"

He pointed a grayish finger with an exposed bone at Duma. "'The Little Rebel Angel,' not happy in Heaven. What does that mean to us humans, huh? What kind of example is that? Hanging around the fringes of Heaven bitching about this and that. Being a misfit. We're all misfits here. But you don't die. You just keep on going bitching and whining and being indecisive, forgetting more memories than I'll ever make. Don't you see how for granted you take your moments. You sons of bitches… the frailty… the finality… you've lost sight of that or maybe you never had it. You make me sick. I'd don't even know why I'm here, and I have larvae and maggots squirming inside me. My vision is blurring and I just want to go home. I just want to go to my wife and make her happy, that's all I want. If you're going to keep me locked up in this wasted body or not take me back to Heaven then at least do something…"

He picked up the book Maggie had given him and threw it against the wall. "It's just *words*."

The audience was silent.

"Damn you all. I just want to see my wife," Honeybone said. "All this other stuff is beyond me."

"We need to get the Book of Life back to Heaven. Not rescue Sopheriel Memeth," Lucifer said. "If we do not, there is a very great chance that there will not be a Heaven. And I say this to a man on the edge of death."

Silence.

"Then I guess you need to do something about it," Honeybone said. "I'm leaving."

Yeshundra opened the door for Honeybone, and shut it behind him.

They stood in silence for a long moment, before Yeshundra reached into a closet and pulled down a small wooden box. He began to fold the flesh of Kirkland up into a neat rectangle.

Maggie turned away, the thumping in her chest becoming alarmingly painful. She sat down and took a small sip of wine. The pain eased as she concentrated on breathing.

Lucifer helped Yeshundra place Kirkland's remains in the box. "The Book?"

"I suggest you follow Mr. Honeybone," Yeshundra said. "I sold the Book to his wife."

∞

Lucifer looked over his shoulder. "Let's go."

"I need rest," Maggie said. "Let's go in the morning."

"We leave now."

"Hold your horses. I need rest. We know where Honeybone is going. He's not going to stray from there," she said. "Give that poor fella a few private hours with his thoughts."

"Very well. Yeshundra?"

"I'll fix up the spare rooms."

∞

Maggie dozed, never quite penetrating the membrane into deep sleep. Every time she closed her eyes, she saw her brother; slaughtered, but standing, like Honeybone. Muscle, sinew, tendons and meat hanging freely as though from a butcher's window. He held up his hands, fingers crushed and dripping with paint.

Why hast thou forsaken me?

She held up her own hands gnarled with arthritis, mirroring him.

The wonders of the world have been made known to you. The nature of God, the nature of free will, your origin and it is not enough.

Flesh and blood...

We are...

My flesh...

Drink of my blood...

Eat of my flesh...

Blood...

Flesh...

Would you die for me?

Flesh and blood.

∞

She awoke quietly, bobbing to the surface of the waking world like an errant diver's marker. At first she thought it was the wind rustling in the curtains, or leaves scraping against the door. She lifted her head just enough to make out two humanoid shapes in the darkness.

"Victor?" she whispered.

They talked quietly in the language she'd come to recognize as Hebrew. Metal softly scraped on metal. She caught the outline of a crooked angel wing.

"Duma?"

The figure whispered something to the other and approached her bed, kneeling down. She could barely make him out in the soft light. Armor adorned his body and an ornate but sleek helmet adorned his head.

"What's going on?"

"Maggie McCreedy, this is Cassiel of the Host."

The other figure stepped beside Duma. She almost didn't recognize him with his armor on. She thought of the scene she'd seen beyond the hills of Eden, but said nothing.

He nodded toward her and she returned it.

"Cassiel has brought my sword and armor."

"I understand," Maggie said.

"You were right. Sopheriel Memeth is of the Host. I am of the Host. He is my brother."

"So you are going—"

"To Hell," Cassiel said.

Duma embraced Maggie. "We will return as soon as possible. If we succeed."

Maggie closed her eyes and held him tightly. "Godspeed, Little One."

TWENTY-TWO: *SNOW WHITE*

HONEYBONE COULDN'T find a cab and realized he had no money anyway. Provided he could even scrape up the necessary change, he didn't want to risk the bus due to the possible number of passengers and well, his stench. He couldn't tell, of course, but a few people he passed on the street made noises in the back of their throats.

Finally, Honeybone wised up and went to the back alley behind a thrift store and rooted around until he found a cap and scarf that would hide his rotting face. He dropped two fingers digging around in the Dumpsters for some lightweight gloves as well. The weather wasn't really appropriate for the clothing, but he didn't care. He turned south down the main road with his head down, and started walking to his wife.

∞

Julianne Grace Honeybone took another bite of mint chocolate chip ice cream as she looked down in vain to see the scale reading. Her swollen belly blocked her view, and for that she was a little grateful. So much so, in fact, that she wolfed down the rest of the ice cream. She stepped off the scale and took a roll of masking tape from the bathroom drawer and ripped off a length and placed it over the digital readout. She then flipped the scale over and popped open the black plastic cover; took the battery out and dropped it into the trashcan under the sink.

Then she took a marker and carefully scribed a "119" on the tape readout. She stood up, back aching and breathing hard from the effort, but pleased with the minor victory.

She leaned back, trying to stretch out some of the ache, when the sharp pain hit her head. She swatted the ice cream container off the counter.

Too cold, too fast.

She leaned on the counter, gritting her teeth, waiting for the pain to subside. The pregnant woman in the mirror looked back at her. She thought she looked like something from Captain Ahab's fantasies. Getting worse, she thought. A rash of acne peppered her forehead. She ran her hand across it. It felt like greasy Braille; this quickly and predictably ousted her elation with replaced it with depression.

Next month.

Just us.

"Damn you, Andy," she said, weakly and grabbed for a tissue. But the tears did not come, so she blew her nose and lumbered back into the bed room, where she took one of Andy's yellow legal pads. She flopped onto the bed and opened her book.

It was a baby name book, and a unique one at that. She'd bought it at a book fair the day her husband had disappeared. Her birthday had been the week before and Andy, in addition to a number of gifts, had given her some cash for books.

It was a tradition back from their salad days. They'd met in a library and it was love at first sight, although it took her a while to finally fully believe she was lucky enough for such a romantic encounter to happen to her. She had joked that she was too poor to buy her own books and called the library her own private collection— on loan to the public, of course.

The next week, he gave her a card with a twenty tucked inside it.

"Just a charitable donation to the library," he'd joked.

She'd bought this book with her latest birthday money.

The two events formed a weird association in her mind and she thought of the book as a gift from beyond the grave. She held it close and took in its smell. Old leather and something else, she couldn't quite place— some floral scent, she thought, but then dismissed it as one of those weird pregnancy things, like the bizarre dreams she'd been having since she conceived.

Julianne cracked it open to the bookmarker. The book listed a most unusual assortment of names; some were utterly ridiculous, some exotic and musical. She continued to read the names, jotting a few here and there. She'd divided the sheet into four sections: One each for girls and boys; then names she loved, and names she considered unique and worthy of further consideration, even if it meant maybe some schoolyard ribbing.

She sipped her tea, which had turned cold, and set it on a wooden coaster on her night stand and pulled the down comforter over her body.

Hold together, baby.

She missed her husband. She thought of going downstairs to his basement study, where more often than not she found herself napping on the old couch there. She thought of the couch and of his smell, his laugh. The way he looked at her.

So full of love and genuine gratefulness...

∞

With great effort Honeybone tried to finish his sojourn. But the sidewalk he'd been jogging on every morning for the past three years had turned into a treacherous landscape, its cracks and slight edges of raised concrete threatening to trip him at every step.

Fall to pieces.

He did not even want to think about the soup that now sloshed around in his shoes. Face turned down and arm wrapped around himself, he finally hailed a cab. After he mumbled an address neither driver nor passenger said anything. Honeybone kept his face down. On the floorboard was a blue booklet.

JESUS SAVES in bold letters on the front.

He asked the driver to drop him off at the end of the block. He stepped out gingerly and heard a faint twittering. He looked to the sky and saw several dark clouds rolling in from the east. He stared at them for a moment and started shaking. The driver tapped his horn to get his attention. Honeybone leaned in the window and pulled down his scarf.

"I'm sorry, I have no money."

Color drained from the driver's face. "Forget about it." And then he drove off.

Looking down, he saw that his clothes on his chest

and gut were dark from seepage.

Hold together, baby.

∞

Honeybone took the key from under the potted fern on the back porch and let himself in quietly.

"Snow White," he whispered. "Your prince is here."

He popped into the small bathroom off the kitchen and combed his hair, which thankfully did not come out in too big of a clump. He took a pair of scissors and trimmed his beard and hair neatly over the ears like she liked it; then he took a can of vanilla bathroom fragrance and sprayed his body several times over.

∞

He slowly made his way up the steps, listening intently; a gentle snoring reached his ears, and he smiled. She was deep asleep. And probably for the best, he thought, not without a touch of sadness. He stopped on the stairs and looked at a cross hanging on the wall. It was from his funeral.

BELOVED HUSBAND AND FATHER.

He fought back a tear and the sobbing that turned his gut into a knot. He didn't want to wake her. He slipped past the landing into their bedroom. She lay there, a dome of down comforter over her swelling belly. Her alabaster skin blended in perfectly with the white of the blanket; a snowbird nestled under a cover of freshly fallen powder.

He had loved her at first sight. Her Snow White appearance, although disturbing to some, was overpoweringly beautiful to him (as was, thankfully, her personality). She was a giving woman now secure with her looks, having put to bed the childhood tortures and teasing. She was also strong woman who wasn't afraid to be open and a touch vulnerable.

And she loved him Andrew Honeybone.

He thought of his indiscretion at that Christmas party so long ago, and sadly shook his head.

A fool.

He crept to the edge of the bed and knelt down beside her. He watched her breath; the rise and fall of her chest, the low rumbling of her snoring. Gingerly, he pushed a stray lock of silver hair from her face. Her high cheekbones were less prominent with the weight from the pregnancy, and there was a rash of acne across her forehead, and he thought, she's never been more beautiful.

"I love you," he whispered. Then something across the room caught his attention.

A baby crib. They had bought it several months ago, but he hadn't put it together. She had. He inspected it, and noticed a few bolts could be tightened. He picked up a wrench from under the crib and tightened two of them, careful to clean the wrench afterwards. Usually, she would supervise while he did the mechanical things, but she had done a good job with the crib. Then he noticed the pillow.

Pink.

He was going to have a *daughter.*

He went back to the bed. Julianne had shifted. A book was tucked under her arm. Gently he took it.

The book was bound with strange leather and stitched with silver. He opened it. The lettering was blurry, and then sharpened into English. A list of names. He flipped through the pages; the book was slim, but the pages kept flipping, as though they were revolving back in a circle under his thumb. He started to read the names. Started to look up a few, and then snapped the book shut. He didn't want to know.

Julianne shifted. "Andy?" she murmured in her sleep.

He sat down beside her. "I'm here, angel." He gently took her hand, and squeezed. Then leaned over her and gave her a brush of a kiss on the lips.

∞

In her dream, she opened her eyes and saw her husband smiling broadly at her, his eyes wet with tears of joy. "My husband. We've made a daughter."

He nodded.

"I love you more strongly than I have ever loved anything in my entire life, Snow White."

"You have made me whole, my Prince, and nothing you might have done will ever change that."

He lowered his head. With a finger she raised his chin. "And that love you feel for me would have tripled with your daughter. But I will love her for the both of us."

He took a pen and wrote something on it, and tucked it in her hand. "I will watch over the both of you."

"Are you going?"

"Not far and not for long," he said. "I will see you again. Soon."

"But—"

He shushed her with a finger to her lips and kissed her firmly. "Sleep now."

∞

Honeybone watched as she rolled over and started snoring again. He stayed there for several minutes, listening to sounds he had not heard in an eternity. The small rapture of the moment occupied him until a raspy voice behind him spoke.

"Would you give your soul for her?"

TWENTY-THREE: *SACRIFICE*

THE CAB DRIVER stood leaning in the doorway, dark wings filling the entrance. The tips of the wings mashed against the ground, supporting him like feathered stilts. Honeybone was confused for a moment, and then he saw the eyes.

Verrier.

Honeybone stood, automatically placing his body between Verrier and his pregnant wife. He was not afraid.

"Would you give your soul for her?"

Honeybone clutched the Book of Life to his chest.

"I could make you watch as I shred your wife's belly open and eat your unborn… daughter, is it? And take the Book, but there's no sport in that, is there? I would rather you make the decision. Of your own free will."

Honeybone glanced around the room.

"Give me the Book, and I'll let one of them live. Your wife or your unborn daughter." His laugh was a barking hack. The stench of rotting wood filled the room. *"Decide."*

Honeybone turned to the window. A dozen bats thudded against it, sonars twittering.

"The Fallen are everywhere."

He advanced, the wings scraping against the hardwood floor.

"Your wife or your unborn child?"

Honeybone retreated by the bed, reached behind him and pulled open the top drawer of the nightstand. He looked behind him. Sitting on top of a stack of women's magazines were two items:

A large box of wooden matches.

A nickel-plated .38.

∞

Without thinking, Andrew Honeybone grabbed the .38.

Verrier laughed. *"Do you surmise—"*

"Father, forgive me," Honeybone said. And then shot his wife.

Once in the belly.

Once in the head.

Verrier was stunned, but only for a second or two. *"A resourceful monkey, aren't you? I suppose I will have to entertain myself with making you watch me devour her body."*

"Can't you see," Honeybone said. "There is nothing you can do to me."

"You are wrong." Verrier walked up to him, tore the book from his grasp and tucked it away. *"I can leave you here. With the remains."*

Honeybone crumbled at the foot of the bed and buried his head in his hands. Verrier towered over him. *"We are victorious. The Revelation has stopped. The ensuing Second Rebellion will be successful."* He ran his fingers through Honeybone's limp hair. *"Your name will be sung as we destroy the Book. I'll leave you with your soul. Tonight, Purgatory becomes a forever place."*

Honeybone looked up at Verrier. The stench of rotting wood was pungent. He spit in Verrier's face.

The expression on Verrier's face changed from a mocking smile to surprise, and then great sadness. He looked down. A dark knife blade protruded from his chest, rotated and then ripped downward, spilling his black entrails. The demon collapsed on Honeybone, who struggled to free himself. Powerful hands grabbed him under his arms and pulled him free.

Lucifer moved Honeybone aside and sheathed his knife as its pictograms danced. "Stupid demon, if only you had read the blade's other side." He kicked Verrier over onto his back.

The demon's lips moved and blackness poured from its maw. A pained mask settling in. *"I did everything I was told. You said I could come with you…"*

Lucifer then took his knife and removed Verrier's head from his body and tossed it aside. It landed with a thud in the baby's crib. He removed the Book of Life from Verrier's cloak.

Maggie spoke, peaking her head into the room. "What did he just say?"

"Nothing," Lucifer said. "It's time to go back to the Silver City."

Honeybone stared wide-eyed at the horror that was once his bedroom. The smoking gun slipped from his fingers.

Maggie saw the gun and the bloody mess on the bed. "My God, the painting was right…"

Honeybone looked at her uncomprehendingly. Maggie did not elaborate.

Lucifer looked at Honeybone, and then at the bed. His eyes narrowed.

Honeybone reached into the nightstand and pulled out the box of matches; he handed them to Maggie.

With the tip of a wing, Lucifer etched a circle in the hardwood floor and traced a symbol in the air.

Honeybone interrupted him. "Please, the mess…"

Lucifer stopped long enough to collect Verrier's remains and pull them into the circle.

That familiar sensation filled Maggie's gut and they all disappeared.

TWENTY-FOUR: *CITY OF SILVER*

THE TRIO APPEARED outside the Field of Gold during the Ritual of Flight.

The beauty of the place took Maggie's breath away, and she struggled to stay on her feet; Lucifer helped her with a tip of his wing, and Honeybone, still in shock, stuck out his arm.

Dozens of angels swooped and dove above the fields, the light glinting off their golden wings. Slowly, one by one, they stopped their aerobatics and hovered. It spread like a wave until they all just hovered there, a shimmering cloud of gold dust. Maggie thought she could hear the low hum of the beating of their wings, and wished her eyes were not failing so fast.

"It is the Ritual of Flight," Lucifer said, almost matter-of-factly. "Our arrive will shorten it."

"It's beautiful," Maggie said.

"That's why they call it Heaven."

They started walking toward the City on the same dirt trail Lucifer trod before the quest began.

We could be skipping down a trail to see the wizard.

Maggie's head moved as though on a swivel. "I reckon it doesn't get any better than this. I don't think I want to go back..."

Honeybone shook the tail of her jacket. The matches rattled around in their box.

"You must. We had a deal; you have a book to write," Lucifer said, sternly. And then in a lighter tone: "But I will give you a tour before you are sent back. We will return the Book of Life and then you and the lawyer will be on your way and I will get my wish."

"To stay here."

"To die here, yes," Lucifer said. "That is my request."

"I understand now," Maggie said. She took out her pad and pen, but wrote nothing. She just kept walking and looking. "Maybe I could see Harold, or Victor," Maggie suggested.

"Andrew Honeybone," Lucifer said. "I am truly sorry. Your wife's beauty rivaled that of home."

Honeybone gave no reaction.

They walked in silence.

"You did the right thing, as hard as that may be."

Maggie sped up, guiding Honeybone with her.

Two angels broke from the floating pack and swooped down and landed as quiet as whispers in a cathedral.

"Prince Morning Star," the tall angel said. "You are to present the Book of Life immediately to the *beth din* which has been established in lieu of the Sopheriel twins."

"So no word from Duma?"

"No. And it is not expected that we shall have any," the shorter one said.

They are not happy to see him; they look a little nervous, Maggie thought. Whether it was just his presence here— a very uncommon sight, she reminded herself— or something else, was unclear.

"We are to escort you to the First Grand Spire."

"May I have the Book?" the taller one said.

"Who is head of the Council?"

"Uriel, fire of God, Archangel of salvation, regent of the sun, Chief Celestial Angel-Prince also known as Nuriel, Jeremiel, Puruel, Uryan, and Jacob-Israel."

"If you don't mind *I* will hand it to him," Lucifer said.

The two exchanged glances, neither stepping forward, their air of authority deflated. "As you wish."

∞

They were escorted to a huge anteroom in the First Grand Spire.

"It's huge," was all Maggie could muster. She noticed the long spiral staircase near the back leading out of sight. "Where does that go?"

"To Yahweh."

Honeybone ran for the stairs, his footfalls echoing hollowly as he plodded in a loping gait.

Maggie's heart went out to him.

An angel ordered him to stop.

But Honeybone only shambled faster, struggling to keep his momentum. He made it to the stairs. Fell to all fours and started to scramble upwards. He made it to the seventh step before a Throne angel swooped down and lifted him off his feet. He set him back down with his traveling companions.

Maggie took Honeybone's gloved hand in hers.

They were lead to a large anteroom where a raised table made of crystal and marble dominated the space. Five angels sat behind it in ornate wooden chairs. The middle chair was taller than the rest. Its occupant wore a gold band around his forehead.

"That is Uriel," Lucifer said to Maggie sensing her question. "He is presiding."

"Presiding?" Maggie said, puzzled. "Over what?"

"An excellent question."

"Prince Morning Star," Uriel said. "Please approach the *beth din.*"

Lucifer did so, a sly look on his face.

"You have been charged with returning the Book of Life to the Silver City. What say you?"

"I, Prince Morning Star, have completed my quest as directed and humbly present to the *beth din* the Book of Life." He took the Book from his cloak and handed it to Uriel, who passed it the closest Council member on the end. The angel took it and perused it before sliding it to the next. Soon it reached the fifth, who faced the center angel and shook his head.

"What is this?" Lucifer said.

"Prince Morning Star, I find it hard to believe you would come all this way just to present a forgery to the Council."

"*WHAT?*"

"This book is *not* the Book of Life."

"And this is not a matter of jest," Lucifer said, barely able to restrain himself.

The Archangel Uriel rapped a gavel on the table. The wide door behind Maggie and Honeybone swung open.

Mr. Pouge walked in, cleaning his glasses. "Yes, indeed." He passed by Maggie. "'lo there."

"Mr. Pouge, would you examine this book for us?"

"Certainly." He was handed the book. He rubbed his

hands against the cover, felt the texture of the paper. Licked the cover and smacked his lips, eyes rolling up in thought. Finally, he took off his glasses and held the book an inch from his face. He put the book down and adjusted his glasses.

"What say you?"

Mr. Pouge cleared his throat. "The cover is delightfully done, but the stitching, which should be a reverse cross, is a straight stitch with an overback finish. Clearly a forgery. This is most certainly *not* the Book of Life. Not indeed."

"Thank you, Mr. Pouge. You are dismissed."

"Yes, indeed." Pouge exited with a wave to Maggie and Honeybone.

"Prince Lucifer, it is the judgment of this Council that you did not complete the quest as directed, and in addition attempted to deceive us."

"But—"

"And also that you alone are responsible for the demise of Mika'il and as such will not be granted your request. You are to be escorted out of the City. For the *final* time."

The gavel came down on the marble table, splintering the head from the shaft.

And then all Lucifer Morning Star broke loose.

TWENTY-FIVE: *DEVIL'S ADVOCATE*

ALL THE RAGE of angels poured from Lucifer. A mirror reflection of Heaven: bright, cold, and blinding.

The *beth din* stood, their chairs crashing to the ground. Throne Seraphim took flight, weapons drawn.

Lucifer howled up to them. "I have been tricked. I did as I was told and I will NOT leave. I will not sit under a judgment such as this a *SECOND* time."

He glowed, the intensity reaching that of a sun's.

Maggie buried her face in her withered hands.

"Do you hear me, my brothers? I will flood the floors of the First Grand Spire with your blood. Do you hear me? I was created First of the Host, and I am First of the Fallen."

His voice terrified Maggie so that she felt utterly

compelled to look at him. To *know* him. The light burned through her retinas, burning in them a supernova.

"I am the Light Giver, the Light Bringer, the Morning Star and I defy this Council's unjust judgment!"

The Council now stood ready. Dozens of Seraphim and Cherubim circled above Lucifer's head. With a huge thrust of his wings he rose to meet them.

The smell of rotting wood was overpowered by something it took Maggie's nose a moment to recognize. The smell of *fear.*

Lucifer let out a roar and the skylights shattered, raining down a million glass diamonds.

The Host held its breath.

"Excuse me...?"

It was a timid voice, soft and hesitant and no one heard it at first but Maggie.

The angels assumed battle stances.

But the voice was louder this time. "Excuse me."

It was Honeybone. *"EXCUSE ME."* His voice boomed and echoed.

The last of the glass shards fell, ushering in a palpable silence.

"If I may approach the Council." He stepped forward, jagged glass crunching beneath his feet. He walked with his gloved hands up, palms open. Voice authoritative. "My name is Andrew L. Honeybone, and I am a lawyer. I would like to speak on Morning Star's behalf."

"The judgment of this Council has been reached, Andrew Honeybone," Uriel said.

"Yes, it has, and now it is time for an appeal to the Council to reconsider its judgment against Morning Star," Honeybone said. He cleared his throat. "According to the *Law of Heaven*."

Uriel leaned over and whispered something to the angel on his left.

"Yes," Morning Star said, gliding to the chamber floor. "Yes, according to the Law of Heaven."

"Go on."

"You've based your judgment against Morning Star on his failure to complete the quest which was to bring you the Book of Life. And on the charge he deceived you. I can testify to you that there was no deception involved. I have become an unwitting part of this quest for reasons which are just now becoming clear to me. I have seen Morning Star act rashly and, perhaps, irresponsibly, but I have also seen him act with compassion, honor, nobility," Honeybone said. "And remorse."

"What do you mean?"

"Lucifer Morning Star killed Michael, this is true, but he did it in accordance with the instructions he was given. And although unfortunately this paradigm has included some souls who perhaps could have been spared, Morning

Star has followed both the letter and spirit of the agreement. The death of Michael caused him no joy; it was not done out of spite or jealousy or vengeance, despite the, shall we say, history between the two.

"Lucifer was charged to rescue me from Eden. Michael and two others had taken me. It was Michael who acted without Blessing, and Michael who stood between Lucifer and the Book. Yeshundra told Lucifer that he would tell him where the Book was, and so Lucifer followed the instructions. The Book delivered here was the book Lucifer was told to bring back. And he did. I would like to take it one step further by saying that I believe, as do Lucifer and others in our party, that there is a conspiracy between factions of Heaven and Hell.

"We still do not know why the Book of Life was taken from Heaven. Only what it represents, and why it must be brought back."

"Do you have proof of this conspiracy, Honeybone?"

"No, your Councilness. Verrier the Fallen was destroyed, and Sopheriel Memeth is still missing, reportedly in Hell."

"I see."

"But this argument aside, there is another point that we may be missing, the most fundamental point of all, perhaps. And that point can be boiled down to one word."
He paused, faced the audience and then back towards the

council.

"Forgiveness."

Silence.

"The Silver City once lost its brightest star. Please do not let that happen again," Honeybone said. "I am finished."

"Honeybone, your words have been spoken from the heart, and we have heard you. You do your profession well, but the verdict of this Council stands. And as you are well aware, with your knowledge of the Law of Heaven, only a Judgment angel may overturn said decision."

"I AM HERE!"

Honeybone turned.

The Council gasped.

A small angel, even smaller than Duma, entered the chamber. His wings were reduced to raw flesh and stripped feathers; flaps of once perfect skin hung in patches from his body and face. He clutched something to his chest.

The Council angels bowed reverently.

Two angels in scarred and scored battle armor escorted the small angel to the head of the Council. Scalps and black pinfeathers of the Fallen adorned their armor and weapons like primitive trophies. It was Duma and Cassiel.

The small angel spoke, "I am Sopheriel Memeth, and I am here to offer my truthful testimony and reclaim my position as a Judgment angel."

"The charges against you and your twin are of the highest crimes," Uriel said.

"And you know that here in the Presence," Sopheriel Memeth said. "No angel may offer falsehoods."

"Yes," Uriel said. "I am aware."

"Then I will speak. Morning Star, I trust you will have no quarrel with that."

"No," Lucifer said. "Please proceed. I wish to end this and reclaim my Creation-right."

"First," Sopheriel Memeth said, placing the item he was carrying on the desk. It was a book. "This is the Book of Life. The Revelation will unfold as it is written, as is the Word."

TWENTY-SIX: *THE DECISION*

"THE BOOK OF LIFE was taken from the City by myself and my twin, who insisted he had come across evidence of a conspiracy in Heaven to take the Book and destroy it, thus preventing the Revelation. I wanted to go to Mika'il with our concerns, but as we feared the worst, we did not know whom to trust."

"It was then that Lucifer arrived in the Silver City seeking asylum. A pact, suggested by Uriel, was made between the Morning Star and the Presence. Return the Book and you will be granted your heart's desire. But Uriel had no desire for the Book of Life to be returned."

"What?" Lucifer said.

"Silence, Morning Star," Sopheriel Memeth said. "Mika'il did not agree with this, not trusting Morning Star to be forthright if indeed he did find the Book. So he enlisted the aid of two others and together they left the City without Blessing, unknowingly proving they could be trusted. Mika'il was *not* part of the conspiracy, but rather its main target. The primary goal of this conspiracy was to remove Mika'il from the Host. Only then could a Second Rebellion have any chance of success. And of all the Host or Fallen who could possibly defeat Mika'il...?"

All eyes turned to Lucifer.

"A clash of these titans was inevitable. And with Lucifer's wish to die, there would then be none powerful enough to stop the Second Rebellion." Sopheriel Memeth turned the Council. "Isn't that correct, Uriel?"

"You accuse me of masterminding such a plan?" Uriel said.

"Say that you did not," Sopheriel Memeth said.

"I will not stand here and be accused of such a crime against the Presence."

"As a Judgment angel I ask you: did you or did you not set this plan in motion?"

Silence.

Uriel shifted. One of the Council angels leaned over, whispered something to his companion and pointed at Uriel.

Maggie squinted and saw the fuzzy shape of Uriel's golden wings darken to brass then copper then to burnt umber and finally to black.

"I rule in favor of the Morning Star," Sopheriel Memeth said. "Your wish is granted."

"I did not mastermind the plan," Uriel said. His wings expanded proudly to their fullest extent. "But I will tell you who did." He walked from behind the table and up to Lucifer. "The Morning Star orchestrated this eons ago. I was to follow him in the First Rebellion. But instead he charged me to stay here. If the First Rebellion failed then we would have a plan to set in motion from within the City. A plan that would allow for the destruction of Mika'il and the return of the Morning Star. We were all to rule. That is what his plan was. We would kneel to no one but Him, no more kneeling before Man. No more being second to Man."

"Oh brother Uriel, your tongue..." Lucifer looked around the chamber. "Yes, there was a plan. Eons ago. In my youth. But the plan did not— never did it call for the destruction of Mika'il." He turned to Uriel. "That was your doing. You betrayed me by altering the plan. You wanted *neither* of us to return."

Uriel said nothing.

Lucifer shifted his wings. "But that plan was formulated a long time ago. I have changed. I am tired and want nothing more than to come home and die. Of that, I am guilty." He turned to Uriel. "You remind me of myself long ago," Lucifer said. "Who in the Council is with you?"

Silence.

Lucifer put his hand behind Uriel's neck and pulled him close and kissed him deeply.

"They will be punished according to the Law of Heaven," Sopheriel Memeth said.

"It is not enough," Lucifer said, with his hand still on Uriel's neck. "It must be undone."

"What?"

"The destruction of Mika'il," Lucifer said. "It must be undone."

"That is not possible," Uriel said. "I have destroyed him. Another rebellion will happen, and Mika'il will not be here to battle it. The Fall will continue and my long Fallen brothers will Rise to a new Glory."

"Can't you see there is nowhere to go from here?" Lucifer smiled.

"Don't do it, Morning Star," Honeybone said.

Maggie didn't understand what they were talking about.

"My brothers on the Council who have betrayed me," Lucifer said, loudly, theatrically. "I cannot blame you for your actions. But I cannot condone them, and I must condemn Mika'il's death. Do you understand?" He spread his wings, a peacock's prideful display. "And I will not be bested." He turned, his skin shimmering. "Sopheriel

Memeth, I have changed the nature of my wish." He paused, catching the eyes of every angel.

"Let us hear it," Sopheriel Memeth said.

"I wish for the recreation of Mika'il."

The chamber stood stunned.

"So be it," Sopheriel Memeth said.

West of Eden, a wild dog howled.

A star was formed in Heaven and from that star was formed an angel of the Thrones.

And that angel was named Mika'il.

Uriel hung his head and wept.

Three members of the Council did likewise, as their wings darkened to black.

"Pride before a fall," Maggie whispered.

"It seems my history repeats itself," Lucifer said to her. "But see how the guilty react? They weep, for they know what Mika'il will do to them." He grinned broadly.

"I'd like to step outside," Maggie said, gathering her notepads.

Honeybone guided her out by the elbow, followed by Lucifer.

The First of the Fallen turned his face to the sun. "It feels different here, this light. I shall miss it."

"Where will you go now?"

TWENTY-SEVEN: *DUMA'S OFFER*

THEY WATCHED Lucifer Morning Star walk out of the Silver City towards the Edge of Darkness.

Duma came up behind them, now clad in white robes instead of his battle armor. Cassiel trailed behind him, silent.

"I'd like to take both of you to a special place, if you would allow me."

"I'd like to be alone now," Honeybone said. "I won't stray far."

Maggie held out her arm; Duma took it, and led them down to the Field of Gold.

"What happened to Sopheriel Memeth's twin?"

"Sopheriel Mehayye? Cassiel and I could not locate him." Duma stood silent for a moment, lost in thought.

"The Ritual of Flight will be resuming soon. It is quite a sight."

Maggie squinted. Shook her head. "My eyes," she said.

"Close them and I will describe it to you with the warmth of the sun on your face and the breeze flowing through your hair." He took her hand and led her to the center of the field to his favorite spot. They lay down together, their backs to the earth, faces to the sky. He squeezed her hand.

"I've never felt so safe," Maggie said.

"Hold that feeling. Draw on it when you feel scared or alone."

They rested, soothed by the sun and the gentle wind. Maggie felt every ache brought on by age, every heartache brought on by time, slowly fade away. Anxiety and fear became distant foreign feelings. A faint flapping sound reached Maggie's ears.

"It's beginning," Duma whispered.

∞

Phantom tactile sensations haunted Honeybone. The jerking of his hand as the revolver fired.

Once in the belly...

Once on the head...

A knot formed in his distended gut, and he crumpled

to the ground. His knees drew slowly to his chest as every remaining muscle in his body seemed to cramp. His face twisted in anguish, but no sound escaped his blue lips. His arms curled over his head and locked. The knot pulled tighter in his gut, and he tried to cry out for his love. The ground was cold and pulled at him, sapping his consciousness.

God, please...

The remains of his eyelids fluttered open. The world was fuzzy, distorted and full of movement. Waves and waves rolled in front of him. Ripples out to infinity. And then, a disturbance in the rippling. A form. It moved toward him. The fuzziness retreated, and his vision sharpened. The form was familiar, but a shape he had not seen in many months.

"Hello, Andy?"

"Snow White? My princess."

The figure came closer and touched him. His body relaxed, the muscles hot and loose.

"My princess—"

"Is alive."

The image altered, becoming something new; shoulders grew broader, hair shorter, from feminine to masculine. Strong wings reached out to Honeybone and scooped him up as lightly as a newborn. A finger caressed his cheek, and his sight was restored. He stared at the angel for a moment, disoriented. A round indention next to the angel's right eye caught his attention. He looked down. Another on his abdomen.

"She and your daughter live."

"They live?"

The angel cradled Honeybone and carried him towards the Field of Gold.

"I know you, you are—"

"Ramiel of the Throne, presider over true visions, chief of thunder, one of five who lead the souls of men to judgment, also named Remiel, Phanuel and Yerahmeel."

"You were there in Eden, you were the third angel. You comforted me. But my wife—"

"In Eden, as you hanged from your feet, you talked of nothing, but your wife and unborn child. I chose to watch over her until she was safe. I did not realize that I would find the Book there. When I did I was taken by surprise, but with Mika'il's death, and Cassiel missing, I thought it best to stay there until contacted. When the Fallen descended on your house, I took her form. She was safely napping down in your study."

"I shot *you*. Not her."

"Yes."

"But the words I spoke to her."

"As Sopheriel Mehayye sent visions to Maggie's brother, I gave your vision to her dreams. She knows your heart, and hers has lifted."

"I don't know what to say."

"We love Him, because first He loved us."

∞

"And it seems we have a visitor," Duma said, as the Ritual of Flight finished.

A great whooshing whipped Maggie's thin hair around her face.

"Greetings, Mika'il," Duma said.

"Greeting, Duma," Mika'il said. "With the removal of Uriel the number of Thrones is six. Wouldst thou become Seven?"

"Me?" Duma said, not without some surprise. "The Little Rebel, an archangel? Now that would be a yarn, eh, storyteller?"

"It is the highest honor I have to offer. I would not be here if it were not for your bravery in rescuing Sopheriel Memeth."

"I am but an instrument, Mika'il," Duma said "Nothing more."

"Perhaps you have something else in mind. Maybe you would like to become an earthwalker."

Honeybone emerged from the wheat into their clearing.

"There are some who could use your protection."

Duma looked at Honeybone. "Yes, I suppose you are correct." He turned to Cassiel. "I wonder who will rule over Hell now?"

"It remains to unfold, but now it is time to escort your companions to their homes."

∞

Duma found Lucifer sitting on the outer edge of the Field of Gold, sunning himself like a winged lizard.

"The time is upon us, Prince Morning Star."

Lucifer stood and surveyed the distant site of the Silver City and the surrounding fields. "Verrier said Hell is but a taste of Heaven. That is not entirely accurate. The hell of that taste is that the memory of it fades, and over time you cannot remember what Heaven was like— only that it gave you joy. That is why the Presence did not slay Cain. Hell is separation from Yahweh."

"It is time," Duma said.

"But before I go," Lucifer said, stroking Maggie's chin. "How is your vision, Maggie?"

"I can see some shapes, some light, not much of anything else."

"I suppose I should fix that since you have a book to write. One at least, which will not be lost. As long as I'm not portrayed as a 'toad,' as Milton wrote."

"Seems to me there's been a number of bargains altered throughout this little trip." She took out the box of matches. On it, in Honeybone's handwriting, were the words: FOR VICTOR. She pinched a small cluster of matches.

"I reckon I can see fine enough."

She dragged the matches against the box. Sulfur and smoke filled her nose and she coughed, her mouth filling with phlegm, as she touched the tiny torch to her notepad. The pages caught fire. She expected Lucifer's claws to dig into her crooked fingers or for his wings to slap her across the face, their sharp edges laying open her flesh.

Instead Duma stepped between them. Lucifer towered over the misfit angel. Their eyes locked for an eternity.

Lucifer stepped away.

Maggie dropped the box of matches.

Lucifer picked it up and shook it. It rattled like a baby's toy.

"It pales in comparison, Margaret McCreedy," he said. "Honeybone, you wrote this to destroy my life on paper, but you came to my defense against the Council. What happened to your word *forgiveness?* I don't understand."

"And concerning matters of the heart," Honeybone said. "I doubt that you ever will."

Maggie tossed the notepad high in the air. Currents swept and swirled the charred and burning pages around like dry leaves on an autumn afternoon.

TWENTY-EIGHT: *DELIVERIES*

"DUMA, I would like to stay here while you escort McCreedy and Honeybone back to earth," Lucifer said. "I am tired, and pose no threat."

Duma laughed. "You may stay, Morning Star. Cassiel will be at your service should you need something."

∞

Honeybone and Duma walked on the water over the lake. The sky was gray and indifferent.

"I guess it's not such a bad day to die."

"You seem chipper."

"I think they call it peace," Honeybone said, as a small wave rolled over his foot. "I have this memory of a warm, safe place and it makes me feel... I don't know how to describe it."

"That is Heaven," Duma said. "You were just there."

"Really?"

"And you will be returning there."

Honeybone smiled. "Thank you."

They stopped. "My wife and daughter are alive."

"She will be looked after."

He nodded, satisfied. "I guess I will see you soon."

Duma smiled and shook his head. "No, you will not."

And with that Honeybone sank down into the water. They maintained eye contact until the murky blackness of the lake consumed him.

∞

What was his favorite ice cream?

Maggie awoke with a start and a burning sensation in her hand. Her cigar had burned down to her fingers. "Damn it." And then she saw a few glowing particles swirling about the room. She realized with a sense of dread that it was the burning end pages of her Sapphire manuscript. She rushed about with a broom, knocking the embers down and stomping them out.

The effort exhausted her, and she collapsed back onto the couch.

The phone rang.

"Hello."

"Maggie, darling, your favorite person."

"Hello, agent."

"Give me some good news."

Maggie took a deep breath. "I've got to rewrite the last third and I'm going to have to break down and hire an assistant. But tell me you can get that extension and I'll spill the beans about Sapphire's marriage proposal."

Without skipping a beat, her agent said, "deal."

"Sapphire will marry."

Her agent let out a whoop. "I knew it."

"She will marry an ordinary foot soldier named Harold."

"What?"

"It's not negotiable," Maggie said. "And I'm hiring my own assistant, not one of your East Coast sissies." She hung up, and misdialed directory assistance. "Damn eyes." She dialed it again.

"What city, please?" the operator said.

"Chicago, I'm looking for an Andrew and Julianne Honeybone."

∞

Back in the Silver City, Lucifer turned as Duma

approached. "I am so tired, Little One," Lucifer said, and indeed his wings sagged as though tethered with great weights.

"Where is it you wish to go?"

"Cast out of Hell," Lucifer said. "Forced to leave the Silver City again."

"You were not forced the first time."

Lucifer smiled. Took a last look. "There is a place I know that will take me."

Duma nodded. "Come, toad."

TWENTY-NINE: *HE WHO WALKS*

"I SHOULD HAVE SURMISED," Duma said, as they walked under the bright and unforgiving sun over Lake Turkana. "Eden."

They continued until they came to the tree where Honeybone had hung by his feet. A tattered rope still remained. To the left, crocodiles sunned themselves in charcoal mud.

"It will be a lonely place."

"I am not so alone," Lucifer said, gesturing to the reptiles.

A vulture cried overhead.

"So, Little One," Lucifer said. "I gather you will take Uriel's place at the Throne. What a great sight it will be for the Little Rebel to rule over that pompous clique. I wish I could be there to see it."

"No one will," Duma said. He touched the hilt of Lucifer's dagger. "Please, cut off my remaining wing."

Lucifer drew his dagger. "So you will become an earthwalker then, living among *adam*."

"No," Duma said.

With great care, Lucifer removed Duma's sole wing and cast it into the lake. The water bubbled with chaos as crocodiles thrashed and wrestled for the fresh meat. "It is only an appetizer, my babies," Lucifer said.

"I am considering another option."

Lucifer laughed, sensing his thoughts. "Even better." He flipped the knife in his hooked hand and extended it to Duma. "You will require this. It is the Key."

Duma nodded and took the knife. "It is heavy."

"Yes."

A circle burned itself black into the sand and Cassiel appeared.

"Fare thee well, Morning Star," Duma said.

As he stepped into the circle, Duma held the key aloft. "Perhaps I will have second thoughts."

And then they were gone in a silent flash.

THIRTY: *FAMILY*

JULIANNE HONEYBONE rocked her two-month-old as Father Harris elicited a few chuckles from his simile of faith by invoking an old *Peanuts* cartoon in which Charlie Brown continues to try to kick the football while Lucy Van Pelt yanks it away.

The baby shifted its dense weight as the congregation quieted. From the last pew, she had a quick escape route to the lobby in case the baby decided to get vocal— which of course it hadn't, not since she was born.

"Blessed with a quiet one," Maggie said, sitting beside her.

She shifted the baby to her other side, feeling the comforting weight against her breast. She stroked his fine dark hair and inhaled her smell, so distinctive and pleasant, a natural fleshy aroma. Julianne rocked her gently, the sermon forgotten. The baby opened her eyes, little more than blue marbles. The corners of her mouth twitched and she sneezed.

The boy in the front of her turned and looked at the baby. He could have been Andrew at age six.

"Bless you," he said, before his mother swatted him lightly on the butt. He swatted her back and she grabbed him and turned him around.

Julianne felt a smile creep across her face. And then she let out a long sigh. Tiny fingers touched her arm. She felt a tightness in her throat, and tears streamed down her face. She made no effort to wipe them and they dotted her baby blanket like little water bombs. And then she was overcome and began to sob. She gathered her bag and rushed out of the church into a quiet area next to the lobby, where she wept loudly.

These fits happened occasionally. Sometimes in the car on the way to the market, on the way to work, and here in church. But this was the first in a few months. The worst had been at Andrew's funeral. Closed casket.

But she was strong for herself and for her baby, she rationalized. The picnic by Andrew's grave though had been the worst.

It had been a wonderfully bright day, a smooth cloudless sky. She packed a cold lunch basket and took the baby out to the grave to meet her father. She'd hoped for a moment filled with joy and sadness mixed, but instead found profound sorrow and grief. It was then that her baby rolled over and touched her arm, so lightly like a feather; and the grief had disappeared, lost in the smile of the child.

"Excuse me..."

She looked up and smiled through the tears. He was an average looking man, dressed rather casually for church, but smiling with an arresting charisma, accentuated by a worn leather eye patch.

"You dropped this." He held out a cassette tape. In a cursive script the words: SAPPHIRE'S WEDDING. Ch. 7, draft 1.

"Thank you," Julianne said, as she took it. "I transcribe tapes for this writer. This is supposed to be a best seller."

"That's a beautiful baby. May I?"

Julianne nodded, surprising herself.

The man leaned forward, stroked the baby's cheek and then his ear.

She liked his cologne, although it was rather on the feminine side. Flowers or something.

"Her skin—"

"An albino," Julianne said. "She takes after her mother."

"Except her eyes."

"She has her father's. They're blue. Very rare in an

albino."

The man tilted his head. "May I ask her name."

She nodded. "Lyric Decca."

"Lyric is beautiful. Decca?"

"Ten. She's the tenth wonder of the world."

"But aren't there only eight?"

"The ninth was my marriage."

The man smiled, stroked his chin and looked to the stained glass window glowing with the afternoon sun. "It's too nice of a day to be cooped up here. Even for a couple of hours."

"Besides, you can read PEANUTS in the paper." She was amazed she'd said that.

He handed her a tissue, and she dabbed her eyes.

"She has your smile."

"I'm sorry I didn't catch your name."

He held out his hand. "Would you like to go for a walk?"

"Sure." She took his hand and pulled herself up. "But not by the lake," Julianne said. "It's too cold." And then she recognized the smell of lilacs.

OMEGA

OVER LAKE TURKANA, the sun reached its apex. Its reflection danced like brilliant white flames, Lucifer noted, turning the lake to fire. The heat began to cook the earth, intensifying the smell. A pack of vultures, having picked some carcass clean, squabbled among themselves. Morning Star drew in a deep breath of putrid air and settled in under the dying tree.

A crocodile stepped forward hesitantly and slowly circled him. Soon another joined it; then, with a speed beguiling of their size, they seized their prey.

Lucifer sat silent, watching as their powerful jaws tore jagged chunks from his flesh. Being crocodiles they did not care where the meat came from and feasted heartily, Lucifer noted, despite their tears.

∞

In the Ninth Circle of Hell, a misfit demon named Etergus napped lazily, ignoring his torture duties again. Hell was bright this day, lit by an unseen source. As he often did, Etergus stomped flat a patch of ground in the center of the Ring of Thorns and made himself comfortable.

He tried to remember that other place, that place that was warm not entirely unlike this place, but was different. He remembered being not entirely unhappy, and even now he could not name the reasons he had had for leaving. He remembered Lucifer speaking to a third of them and his reasons had seemed sound then, although he was hard pressed to remember them now. He did remember that Little Rebel angel who didn't come with him and who had even cautioned Etergus against joining in the Fall.

He screwed his eyes shut and tried to find that memory in the dank coil of his mind. More than once, he'd almost grasped the memory, only to have it float away just beyond his over-mind...

A creaking louder than the cries of the damned awoke Etergus from his slumber. He shook his head, and rubbed his eyes with his horned fists.

The creaking again.

He sat bolt upright. Over the next hill he could see the

tops of the massive gates of Hell. They were opening.

That can't be right, he thought.

They are locked.

Etergus ran to the top of the hill and shat himself.

He took off running as fast as his many legs could carry him, down the rocky path lined with pikes adorned with small skulls of monkeys. He raced until his body burned with fatigue, but he did not stop. He crossed from the dirt path to the paved stone leading up to the steps of the First Great Spire.

"He's here, he's here!" Etergus screamed.

A demon guard kicked him in the face, knocking him to the bottom of the stairs. "What are you shouting about, pig?" a giant demon said.

"The new *ha-satan* comes."

The demon guard laughed. "That is not possible."

The door to the First Great Spire opened. Flanked by several guards was Verrier, his body a patchwork of several demon 'volunteers'. He held a leash, the end of which was attached to a barbed metal collar around the neck of archangel Sopheriel Mehayye, stripped of flesh and wings, and on all fours.

"Etergus, need I remind you," Verrier said. "I am the new *ha-satan*."

"But my Liege," Etergus said, pointing in the direction of the gates. "He comes."

Verrier scanned the sky. "I see nothing."

"He is not airborne," Etergus said, panting.

"What do you mean?" Verrier said.

"The Gates have opened," Etergus said. "He has the *Key*."

The guard demons broke ranks, stepping away from Verrier who teetered without their support. "By what—what name do we know him?"

Sopheriel Mehayye spoke, his cracked and blood-caked lips parting as a grin formed:

"He Who Walks."

Finis

DAVID SCOTT HAY is an award-winning Chicago playwright and screenwriter. He made his feature debut as writer/director with the kick-ass indie feature *Hard Scrambled* starring Kurtwood Smith (That 70s Show, *Robocop*).

There's a half-dozen plays in there somewhere as well.

He holds an MFA in Fiction/Stage & Screen from Queens University of Charlotte. Novels include *Fountain* a dark comedy/satire, and the best selling fantasy/mystery, *Fall: The Last Testament of Lucifer Morningstar (The Fallen Chronicles: Book One.)*.

He is also a Contributing Editor for *The Digital Americana Magazine* - A Literary & Culture Magazine.

He lost the tip of a finger in chop-saw incident.

Twitter: @DavidScottHay
david@davidscotthay.com
www.davidscotthay.com

Coming Winter 2012

HELL'S GATE A US Armored Cavalry regiment gets lost in a freak sandstorm and finds themselves in a strange hellish land... (horror, military, sci-fi) *The Fallen Chronicles: Book Two*